Schizophrenia

Peggy J. Parks

Diseases and Disorders

ReferencePoint Press®

San Diego, CA

ReferencePoint
Press®

© 2011 ReferencePoint Press, Inc.
Printed in the United States

For more information, contact:
ReferencePoint Press, Inc.
PO Box 27779
San Diego, CA 92198
www.ReferencePointPress.com

Picture credits:
Cover: Dreamstime and iStockphoto.com
Maury Aaseng: 31–33, 46–48, 61–63, 76–77
Jerry Cooke/Science Photo Library: 18
Wellcome Department of Cognitive Neurology/Science Photo Library: 10

LIBRARY OF CONGRESS CATALOGING-IN-PUBLICATION DATA

Parks, Peggy J., 1951–
    Schizophrenia / by Peggy J. Parks.
        p. cm. — (Compact research series)
    Includes bibliographical references and index.
    ISBN-13: 978-1-60152-140-8 (hardback)
    ISBN-10: 1-60152-140-5 (hardback)
    1. Schizophrenia—Juvenile literature. I. Title.
    RC514.P295   2011
    616.89'8—dc22

                                                            2010037253

Contents

Foreword

As modern civilization continues to evolve, its ability to create, store, distribute, and access information expands exponentially. The explosion of information from all media continues to increase at a phenomenal rate. By 2020 some experts predict the worldwide information base will double every 73 days. While access to diverse sources of information and perspectives is paramount to any democratic society, information alone cannot help people gain knowledge and understanding. Information must be organized and presented clearly and succinctly in order to be understood. The challenge in the digital age becomes not the creation of information, but how best to sort, organize, enhance, and present information.

ReferencePoint Press developed the *Compact Research* series with this challenge of the information age in mind. More than any other subject area today, researching current issues can yield vast, diverse, and unqualified information that can be intimidating and overwhelming for even the most advanced and motivated researcher. The *Compact Research* series offers a compact, relevant, intelligent, and conveniently organized collection of information covering a variety of current topics ranging from illegal immigration and deforestation to diseases such as anorexia and meningitis.

The series focuses on three types of information: objective single-author narratives, opinion-based primary source quotations, and facts and statistics. The clearly written objective narratives provide context and reliable background information. Primary source quotes are carefully selected and cited, exposing the reader to differing points of view. And facts and statistics sections aid the reader in evaluating perspectives. Presenting these key types of information creates a richer, more balanced learning experience.

For better understanding and convenience, the series enhances information by organizing it into narrower topics and adding design features that make it easy for a reader to identify desired content. For example, in *Compact Research: Illegal Immigration*, a chapter covering the economic impact of illegal immigration has an objective narrative explaining the various ways the economy is impacted, a balanced section of numerous primary source quotes on the topic, followed by facts and full-color illustrations to encourage evaluation of contrasting perspectives.

The ancient Roman philosopher Lucius Annaeus Seneca wrote, "It is quality rather than quantity that matters." More than just a collection of content, the *Compact Research* series is simply committed to creating, finding, organizing, and presenting the most relevant and appropriate amount of information on a current topic in a user-friendly style that invites, intrigues, and fosters understanding.

Schizophrenia at a Glance

Schizophrenia Defined

Schizophrenia is a severe disorder of the brain that distorts someone's ability to perceive reality.

Types of Schizophrenia

The three main types of schizophrenia are paranoid, disorganized, and catatonic schizophrenia.

Symptoms

Symptoms of schizophrenia include delusions, hallucinations, and disorganized thinking accompanied by the absence of normal emotions and behavior.

Prevalence

Schizophrenia affects an estimated 24 million people worldwide, including 2.4 million adults in the United States. This totals about 1 out of every 100 Americans over the age of 18.

Childhood Schizophrenia

Early onset schizophrenia, which strikes children under the age of 12, is extremely rare, affecting from 1 in 30,000 to 1 in 50,000 children.

Causes

Scientists believe that schizophrenia is caused by a complex interaction of genetic and environmental factors.

Treatment Options

Mental health professionals often treat schizophrenia patients with a combination of antipsychotic medications and psychotherapy.

Associated Problems

People with schizophrenia often feel misunderstood and stigmatized by society because of their illness; many develop problems with alcohol and drug abuse.

Overcoming Schizophrenia

Schizophrenia cannot be cured, but medical science has developed treatments that make it possible for many to overcome the disease and live normal lives.

Overview

❝Commonly known as insanity or madness, schizophrenia is a chronic psychotic disorder with onset typically occurring in adolescence or young adulthood.❞

—Paul S. Gerstein, an emergency medicine and family practice physician from Holyoke, Massachusetts.

❝Because we have this tendency to 'listen to a different drummer,' we often experience difficulties in communicating with our more 'normal' friends. Sometimes others perceive what we say and do as strange or bizarre.❞

—Frederick J. Frese, a psychologist and lecturer who overcame paranoid schizophrenia after suffering from it for many years.

In a September 2008 *Newsweek* article, Dr. Donald C. Goff directed his words at teenagers. As a psychiatrist and the director of the schizophrenia program at Massachusetts General Hospital, Goff knows how frightening the paranoid thoughts that often accompany the disease can be. He shared a hypothetical scenario to help kids understand how schizophrenia seizes control of the mind:

> You're a senior in high school, sitting in math class, when suddenly a voice from the loudspeaker tells you the CIA has killed your parents and replaced them with imposters. Days later you notice strangers watching you. In fact, they are listening to your thoughts. No one can convince you that your ideas are irrational and, because you don't feel ill, you refuse to see a doctor. Instead, you

tell a friend you will foil the conspiracy by committing suicide. Hours later, the police arrive to take you to the hospital. This is one of the common ways schizophrenia announces itself.[1]

What Is Schizophrenia?

Of all the mental illnesses, schizophrenia is often called the most devastating. It is a chronic, severe brain disorder that distorts the way sufferers think, feel, act, and perceive everyone and everything around them. As the World Federation for Mental Health explains: "Worldwide, the burden of mental illness is great, and multiplied in the many countries fraught with famine, civil war, HIV/AIDS and disaster. Schizophrenia is, by far, the most debilitating yet least understood of all of these illnesses."[2]

Schizophrenia's name has roots in the Greek language: from *schizein*, meaning "to split," and *phreno*, which means "mind." Together, these words aptly define the disease because its primary characteristic is a faulty connection—or split—between reality and what sufferers' minds lead them to believe. The altered reality experienced by people with schizophrenia is known as psychosis, and someone who experiences it is said to be psychotic.

In most people with schizophrenia, the disease develops slowly, with subtle symptoms and a gradual decline in functioning. This is known as the prodromal stage, as Goff explains: "Typically there is a gradual onset of apathy, social withdrawal, deteriorating performance in school or at work and change in personality (the prodrome), which precedes psychosis." Goff adds, however, that the time it takes for schizophrenia to develop can vary considerably from person to person. In some cases, as shown in his example of the teenager whose paranoid thoughts seemed to appear out of nowhere, "onset of psychosis is often pretty sudden."[3] According to a 2006 British study, sudden onset of psychosis (meaning no prodromal phase) occurs in 22.2 percent of schizophrenia cases.

> " Of all the mental illnesses, schizophrenia is often called the most devastating. "

Delusions and Hallucinations

Unlike many diseases that fit into well-defined categories, schizophrenia is not easily characterized. Based on symptoms, it is loosely divided into three major subtypes: paranoid, disorganized, and catatonic. A fourth category, undifferentiated schizophrenia, is diagnosed when someone ex-

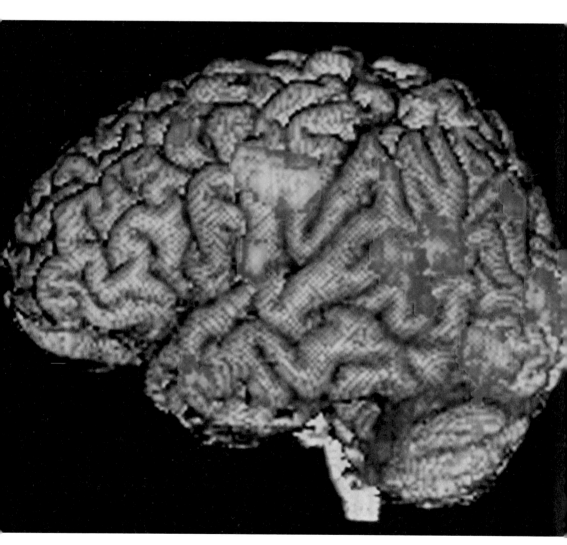

During a hallucination, a scan shows activity (orange) in the visual (at right) and auditory (upper center) areas of a schizophrenic patient's brain. Increased activity in certain areas of the brain may correspond with schizophrenic hallucinations.

hibits symptoms of schizophrenia over a period of time but does not fit the criteria of any one subtype.

Schizophrenia symptoms are also categorized by type, with one category referred to as positive. In the context of schizophrenia, *positive* does not refer to *good*, but rather to characteristics that are abnormal and should not be there. Delusions are the most common of all positive symptoms, with an estimated 90 percent of schizophrenia sufferers experiencing them at some stage of their illness. People with delusions have strange, irrational beliefs about events or circumstances that they feel certain are real.

Although most people with schizophrenia experience some form of delusions, they are the hallmark of paranoid schizophrenia. Those who suffer from the paranoid form are often extremely suspicious of others, even their own friends and family members. They become convinced that everyone is "out to get them" or believe that they are being plotted against. The Mayo Clinic explains: "In paranoid schizophrenia, delusions are often focused on the perception that you're being singled out for harm. Your brain misinterprets experiences and you hold on to these false beliefs despite evidence to the contrary. For instance, you may believe that the government is monitoring every move you make or that a co-worker is poisoning your lunch."[4]

> When people mistakenly assume that those who suffer from schizophrenia have multiple personalities, they are confusing it with a rare mental illness known as dissociative identity disorder.

Nearly as prevalent as delusions are hallucinations, which are also considered positive symptoms. Hallucinations are things that schizophrenia sufferers see, hear, smell, or feel, but which do not actually exist. These are most often auditory hallucinations, whereby the person hears voices that no one else can hear. People with schizophrenia have described these voices as threatening, terrifying, or abusive, ordering them to commit harmful acts or injure themselves or others. Dean A. Haycock, author of *The Everything Health Guide to Schizophrenia*, writes: "This alone can be disorienting and terrifying. Imagine living with voices originating inside your head. Whose voices are they? Why do they say such demeaning, disturbing, and demoralizing things? Why won't they stop?"[5]

When Thinking Gets Disrupted

Disorganized schizophrenia is often said to be the most severe form of the disease. It typically appears at a younger age than paranoid schizophrenia and causes a serious disruption of thought processes known as disorganized (or disordered) thinking. Another of the positive symptoms, disorganized thinking involves fragmented thoughts that render schizophrenia sufferers unable to think or speak in a logical fashion, which leads to speech that is incoherent and all but impossible to follow. The National Institute of Mental Health explains: "They may talk in a garbled way that is hard to understand. Another form is called 'thought blocking.' This is when a person stops speaking abruptly in the middle of a thought. When asked why he or she stopped talking, the person may say that it felt as if the thought had been taken out of his or her head."[6]

Many with disorganized thinking intersperse conversation with nonsensical words and statements. They may speak in neologisms, or made-up words, that make sense to no one but the individual who uses them. Also typical is a pattern of repetition in which the person says the same things over and over again—stringing together neologisms, words, and phrases into incoherent gibberish known as a "word salad." Another common trait is exhibiting inappropriate emotion, such as acting silly and laughing after being told about the death of a good friend.

> No two people with schizophrenia undergo the exact same treatment, because what works well for some may not be effective for others.

Although disorganized thinking is a positive symptom, people with disorganized schizophrenia may also display negative symptoms. These are characteristics and behaviors that should be there but are noticeably absent, as Haycock explains: "Negative symptoms are 'subtractions' from normal functions. They represent severely diminished or missing traits.

Although most people think of delusions or auditory hallucinations when they think of schizophrenia, negative symptoms are just as much a part of the disease."[7] Characteristic of this is a flat affect, meaning the sufferer appears to lack emotion or feelings. Schizophrenia sufferers who have this trait typically avoid eye contact, their faces are blank and expressionless, and if they speak their voices have a dull, monotonous tone.

Mental health professionals often say that negative symptoms are worse than positive symptoms because of how seriously they can impair someone's quality of life. People who suffer from negative symptoms often have no interest in the world around them. They lose all sense of enjoyment and lack the ability to feel pleasure or act spontaneously. They may reach the point of completely avoiding interaction with family and friends, have no desire ever to leave their homes, and totally neglect personal hygiene.

A Disease of Extremes

The catatonic type is the rarest form of schizophrenia; few cases have been reported in the United States and other Western countries. As New York psychiatrist Lynn E. DeLisi writes: "A currently practicing young U.S. psychiatrist may never have seen such cases."[8] Behaviors associated with catatonic schizophrenia can vary wildly from patient to patient. At one end of the spectrum, those who suffer from it may be mute and unresponsive, seemingly unable to talk even when they are spoken to. They may be completely immobile, with their limbs fixed in an odd position for hours at a time. DeLisi explains: "Patients with classical catatonia are often quite remarkable in their appearance. They have what has been termed 'waxy flexibility.' That is, they stand in one position with their limbs stationary until a person moves them to another position, where they will stay until again moved by another person."[9]

Not all people with catatonic schizophrenia are mute and immobile—some exhibit behavior that is quite different. Sufferers who are in a state known as hyperactive or agitated catatonia may exhibit extreme excitability, agitation, and frenzied behavior. They may shout, talk rapidly, and pace back and forth as they speak. They may also exhibit mimicry, as Haycock writes: "The person copies what someone else says or does and repeats the words or actions incessantly. If the patient parrots a word, she is said to show echolalia. If she repeatedly imitates someone's physical movements, she is said to have echopraxia."[10]

Prevalence of Schizophrenia

Schizophrenia strikes people of all ages and from all walks of life, as the National Alliance on Mental Illness explains: "It's an illness that is twice as common as HIV/AIDS. It does not discriminate. It strikes people of all races and both genders, and cuts across all social and economic classes."[11] According to the World Health Organization, about 24 million people worldwide suffer from schizophrenia. In the United States the disease affects an estimated 2.4 million adults.

Although both males and females suffer from schizophrenia, the age of onset differs slightly. According to Goff, the disease usually strikes males when they are in their late teens or early twenties, and females in their mid- to late twenties. When symptoms appear after the age of 40, this is known as late-onset schizophrenia, with very-late-onset schizophrenia affecting adults who are 60 and older. Schizophrenia among older adults is thought to occur much less often than in younger people, but few studies have been done to quantify this. As psychiatrists Jessica Broadway and Jacobo Mintzer explain: "Schizophrenia in the elderly has been largely disregarded by researchers. Over 90% of published papers on schizophrenia have excluded elderly persons with the disorder."[12]

Early onset schizophrenia, which affects children under the age of 12, is exceedingly rare. According to Judith Rapoport, who is chief of the National Institute of Mental Health's child psychiatry division, children develop schizophrenia at only 1/300th of 1 percent of the rate for adults. Rapoport says that the onset of schizophrenia almost always happens gradually in a child, as she explains: "Over a period of months, the children may start to lose interest in friends or activities, and they may start to have some very strange behaviors like running out of the house in the middle of the night undressed or start to say very strange things to their parents about not trusting them, talk about being poisoned."[13]

The Multiple Personality Myth

Mental health professionals say that schizophrenia is one of the most misunderstood of all mental illnesses; it is often mistakenly characterized as a disorder that causes people to have multiple personalities. Elyn R. Saks, who is a professor of law, psychology, and psychiatry at the University of Southern California, has intimate knowledge of schizophrenia because she struggled with it for much of her life. She writes: "Whatever schizophrenia is, it's not 'split personality,' although the two are often confused by the public; the schizophrenic mind is not split, but shattered."[14]

When people mistakenly assume that those who suffer from schizophrenia have multiple personalities, they are confusing it with a rare mental illness known as dissociative identity disorder. Although people who have that disorder do exhibit two or more different personalities—an average of 10 according to the National Alliance on Mental Illness—it is entirely separate from schizophrenia.

What Causes Schizophrenia?

Through years of research, scientists have learned that schizophrenia is the product of brain chemistry gone awry, but why this happens is a mystery. Neurologist and schizophrenia researcher Paul Thomson explains: "Schizophrenia is so horrendously complicated from a scientific point of view that everything one says has to be qualified. This is true for all the mental illnesses. There's simply no agreed-upon physical marker in the brain for what causes them. There are various theories, but even the most basic information is a matter of debate."[15]

Studies have shown that there is a strong hereditary component in schizophrenia, with a family history being the most significant risk factor for someone to develop it. Where there is no family history, schizophrenia affects about 1 percent of the adult population, with the likelihood rising to 10 percent if a parent or sibling has it. The risk is highest among twins: According to the National Institute of Mental Health, if one identical twin has schizophrenia, the other has a 40 to 65 percent chance of also developing it.

> " Living with schizophrenia can be excruciatingly painful for those who suffer from it, as well as for their families and friends. "

Yet genetics alone cannot explain schizophrenia. If genes were solely responsible, every person who is predisposed to the disease would develop it, and most never do. Rapoport explains: "There is a lot of information on risks for schizophrenia, generally, that includes children and adults. It's a bewildering array, suggesting that first of all, it's in part genetic, but only part. Identical twins are only both ill in a little less than half the cases, and since they have the same genes, that means you need something else in order to have the disorder."[16] Rapoport's reference to "something else" refers to environmental factors, such as stressful life events. Also, the prenatal environment (where a fetus develops in the mother's womb) is believed to play a role in the development of schizophrenia. Scientists say that prenatal exposure to environmental toxins or viruses, prenatal malnutrition, or complications during labor and delivery increase the risk that a child will develop schizophrenia later in life.

A Schizophrenia Diagnosis

Schizophrenia can be challenging for mental health professionals to diagnose. One reason is that its symptoms are often similar to those of other mental illnesses such as bipolar disorder (which involves severe mood swings) and depression. Schizophrenia can be especially difficult to diagnose in teenagers, as the National Institute of Mental Health explains: "This is because the first signs can include a change of friends, a drop in grades, sleep problems, and irritability—behaviors that are common among teens."[17]

Before schizophrenia can be diagnosed, a physician does a complete physical examination. Typically he or she will order a series of tests to check for medically related problems such as neurological conditions, thyroid problems, hypoglycemia (low blood sugar), kidney disease, or substance abuse. Once medical conditions have been ruled out, a psychiatrist will likely conduct a complete mental status workup. This involves observing the patient's behavior, as well as interviewing family members to collect information about the events that led up to the current problem.

How Schizophrenia Is Treated

No two people with schizophrenia undergo the exact same treatment, because what works well for some may not be effective for others. Treating the illness often involves experimenting with different medications to find the ones that alleviate the patient's symptoms without causing severe side effects. Antipsychotic drugs are often prescribed for those who suffer from hallucinations and delusions. These drugs correct an imbalance in the chemicals that enable brain cells to communicate with each other, and they have proved to be a breakthrough in schizophrenia treatment.

For many schizophrenia patients, medications are only part of the recommended treatment regimen. According to psychiatrists Jerome and Irene S. Levine, psychotherapy is also important, as they explain: "It would be wonderful if all the symptoms and signs of schizophrenia could be whisked away by merely swallowing a pill. Unfortunately, even the best medications alone aren't a cure-all." Although drugs can be invaluable for treating and controlling schizophrenia symptoms, the Levines say it is psychotherapy that helps sufferers regain their sense of self-worth and their ability to function in society.

> " **Even though schizophrenia cannot be cured, it is a treatable illness for which there is more hope than ever before.** "

They write: "The losses associated with an acute episode of schizophrenia can be devastating. Medication—although it can usually help stabilize symptoms so life is more 'normal'—can't erase the pain of feeling stigmatized, left out, and unable to cope with tasks that seem to come easily to peers, such as living independently or holding down a job."[18]

What Problems Are Associated with Schizophrenia?

Living with schizophrenia can be excruciatingly painful for those who suffer from it, as well as for their families and friends. Because schizophrenia sufferers are out of touch with reality and exhibit bizarre behavior such as hearing and seeing things that do not really exist, people may be frightened of them and intentionally keep their distance. This can make someone with schizophrenia feel isolated and alone, as well as ashamed of symptoms over which he or she has no control.

Another problem for schizophrenia sufferers is the perception that they are violent and dangerous. Organizations such as the National Alliance on Mental Illness and the Schizophrenia and Related Disorders Alliance of America state that people with schizophrenia are no more prone to violence that those who do not have the disease. This issue is contro-

Schizophrenia was once viewed as untreatable and those who suffered from it were locked away in institutions for the insane. Medical science has vastly improved that bleak outlook, captured in this 1946 photograph at an Ohio insane asylum.

versial, however. Some studies have shown that people with schizophrenia are two to three times more likely to commit violent crimes than those who do not have the disease.

Can People Overcome Schizophrenia?

In the past, people with schizophrenia were typically written off as insane and untreatable. Most were shunned by society and locked away in institutions, with no chance of ever being released or getting better. Even as recently as the 1980s, patients were told that they had little or no chance to live a normal life, as was Saks's experience when she was diagnosed with schizophrenia. She writes: "Repeatedly I ran up against words like 'debilitating,' 'baffling,' 'chronic,' 'catastrophic,' 'devastating,' and 'loss.' For the rest of my life. *The rest of my life*. It felt more like a death sentence than a medical diagnosis."[19]

Fortunately, medical science has vastly improved that bleak outlook. Even though schizophrenia cannot be cured, it is a treatable illness for which there is more hope than ever before—and Saks herself is living proof of that. Although she still faces challenges, she has largely overcome the disease that once threatened to hold her mind hostage forever. She writes: "My life today is not without its troubles. I have a major mental illness. . . . I will always have good days and bad, and I still get sick. But the treatment I have received has allowed me a life I consider wonderfully worth living."[20]

What Is
Schizophrenia?

66Of all the ways in which the brain can become damaged, schizophrenia remains the least understood and the most frightening.99

—Donald C. Goff, director of the schizophrenia clinical and research program at Massachusetts General Hospital and a psychiatry professor at Harvard Medical School.

66While depression is often referred to by mental health professionals as the 'common cold' of mental illness, schizophrenia is considered the 'cancer.' This is because it is probably the most serious and debilitating psychiatric disorder that exists.99

—Cheryl Lane, a clinical psychologist who writes for the mental health Web site Schizophrenic.com.

Dr. Cyndi Shannon Weickert is a neurobiologist who heads a schizophrenia research program in Sydney, Australia. When she was a young girl, she dreamed of someday becoming a famous chef—but that changed when her twin brother, Scott Shannon, developed schizophrenia. As Weickert watched him lose his grasp on reality, a commitment took shape in her mind. She writes: "Seeing my twin brother suffer with this illness and the horrifying side effects of his inadequate treatment motivated me to dedicate my life to research the underlying cause of this devastating disorder, ultimately to develop better and more rational treatments."[21]

Weickert first began to notice changes in her brother's behavior when they were teenagers, and she saw him "starting to withdraw and descend into a scary and strange new world."[22] One of the first warning signs was when he positioned coat hangers around his bedroom to serve as antennae so he could receive "messages" meant only for him. At their seventeenth birthday party, he began rambling incoherently, accusing his sister of being the devil's daughter and claiming that he possessed knowledge of dark and evil things that were happening in the world. But the most frightening incident occurred when Shannon turned on his mother, throwing her up against the wall and threatening to harm her. Normally a gentle, loving person, for him to undergo such a frightening personality change was an ominous sign that he was very sick—which he was. A psychiatric evaluation confirmed that he had schizophrenia.

> **Scott Shannon had a perfectly normal childhood and a happy home life, was close to his family, and did well in school. Then, unexplainably, he developed schizophrenia.**

Shannon fought his disease for more than 20 years, a period that included hospitalizations and trying a variety of antipsychotic medications. Many of those medications caused horrible side effects such as uncontrollable movements of his mouth and tongue. By the time Shannon finally found a drug that helped ease his symptoms, he had gained an excessive amount of weight, suffered from diabetes, and had a weakened heart. On Thanksgiving Day 2008, his long battle with schizophrenia ended when he had a heart attack and died at his family home. His death was a terrible blow to Weickert. Even though she takes comfort in knowing that her career is devoted to helping people like her brother, losing him was traumatic. She writes: "I miss him dearly. I loved Scott so much, and I wish I could have done more to improve his life. . . . One day I hope we will have answers to prevent and cure this terrible disease."[23]

Crushed Hopes and Dreams

Scott Shannon had a perfectly normal childhood and a happy home life, was close to his family, and did well in school. Then, unexplainably, he developed schizophrenia. The same was true of Bill Garrett, a young man from Maryland. In high school Garrett achieved such high academic honors that he won a four-year scholarship to Johns Hopkins University. He was captain of the school's lacrosse and cross-country teams, as well as student government president. Most everyone who knew him fully expected that he would achieve great things in his life—but that changed when he developed schizophrenia. His sister Nickole explains: "I watched the big brother who I had looked up to all my life fall apart and become someone entirely new. The boy who was destined for greatness, who worked long and hard for 12 years to lead a successful life, was destroyed in a mere six months."[24]

Garrett's psychosis began just as he was starting college, and its onset was sudden. Without warning, voices filled his head, and he could hear them taunting him: "They're coming for you. Find somewhere to hide, they're going to get you."[25] The voices were relentless. They told Garrett that he was fat and that he was stupid. They made him believe that his father had poisoned the family dog, Nickole had injected his pet lizard with methamphetamine, and his grandmother was putting human body parts in his food.

> "
> **Garrett tried numerous antipsychotics, but the side effects were unbearable. Some drugs made him sleepy, one caused him to gain 75 pounds (34kg), and others made him turn violent.**
> "

As psychotic delusions continued to plague Garrett, his grades plummeted, and he was forced to leave college and move back home. Once an avid reader who possessed hundreds of books, he could no longer read because the voices drowned out the words. He stopped washing and showering because the voices told him the soap and shampoo were poisoned. He told his mother that the one thing he looked forward to was sleeping because that was the only time the voices left him alone.

Garrett tried numerous antipsychotics, but the side effects were unbearable. Some drugs made him sleepy, one caused him to gain 75 pounds (34kg), and others made him turn violent. Finally, doctors found a drug that seemed to help him, and he started to show signs of improvement. He was able to interact with his family, including carrying on conversations with them. Yet even now Garrett knows that the future is uncertain and his illness will undoubtedly place many hurdles in his path. One day in a moment of hopelessness, he said to his mother: "I was on the top of the world. Now I'm in the gutter."[26] Only time will tell whether he will be able to overcome his schizophrenia and again climb back to the top of his world.

The Nightmare of Psychosis

Since most cases of schizophrenia develop during the late teens or early adulthood, subtle warning signs may appear during adolescence. If symptoms are taken seriously rather than ignored, this could potentially lead to an early diagnosis and a better outcome for the patient. But identifying schizophrenia in teenagers can be challenging, as Elyn R. Saks writes: "The problem is that prodromal symptoms, viewed separately or together, mirror what many healthy teenagers experience in their routine passage through adolescence: sleep irregularities, difficulty in concentrating, vague feelings of tension or anxiety, a change in personality, and perhaps a withdrawal from the social life of their peers."[27]

Saks was not diagnosed with schizophrenia until she was in her twenties. But as she looks back on her life, symptoms such as phobias and night terrors were starting to develop when she was a child. By the time she was a teenager, she was having hallucinations and delusional thoughts. She became convinced that houses she passed while walking were sending her ominous messages, telling her that she was special, then telling her she was especially bad. She writes: "I didn't hear these words as literal sounds, as though the houses were talking and I were hearing them; instead, the words just came into my head—they were ideas I was having. Yet I instinctively knew they were not *my* ideas. They belonged to the houses, and the houses had put them in my head."[28]

> " Since most cases of schizophrenia develop during the late teens or early adulthood, subtle warning signs may appear during adolescence. "

Saks continued to suffer from psychosis throughout college, as well as during graduate school in England. Somehow she managed to hide her illness from most classmates and acquaintances—but that changed when she had a psychotic breakdown during her first year of law school. Saks was studying in the library with several other students when she suddenly launched into a nonsensical rant: "Memos are visitations. They make certain points. The point is on your head. Pat used to say that. Have you ever killed anyone?" Then she jumped up from her chair, climbed through a window onto the roof, and began waving her arms around and hollering, "This is the real me!" and in a loud voice she sang: "Come on, let's dance! Come to the Florida sunshine bush. Where they make lemons. Where there are demons."[29]

Saks's outburst shocked and frightened the other students. After she came back inside they called off their study date and left the library, while Saks sat alone, shaking uncontrollably. Later, back in her apartment, she was filled with shame over what she had done. She sat on her bed, rocking back and forth and moaning to herself, feeling isolated and afraid. She writes: "I had finally done it: cracked in public, in front of colleagues, my law school classmates. Who I was, what I was, had been revealed. Now everyone would know the truth—of my worthlessness, my evil. . . . Something was prying my grip loose, finger by finger, and very soon now, I was simply going to fall through space."[30] Even then, Saks did not know that she had schizophrenia—nor did she have any way of knowing what a long and painful road she would have to travel before overcoming it.

The Tortured Mind of a Child

For a child to be stricken with schizophrenia is exceptionally rare, with estimates ranging from 1 in 30,000 to 1 in 50,000, compared with 1 in 100 adults. And when the disease does affect children, their suffering is especially brutal, as Nitin Gogtay, a neurologist at the National Institute of Mental Health, explains: "Child-onset schizophrenia is 20 to 30 times more severe than adult-onset schizophrenia. Ninety-five percent of the time they are awake these kids are actively hallucinating. I don't think I've seen anything more devastating in all of medicine."[31]

Jani Schofield is one of those rare children. Just before her third birthday, she began to talk about an imaginary cat she called Low. Her parents thought nothing of it because they knew kids often have imaginary playmates. Soon Jani was talking about hundreds of imaginary creatures, such as an orange tabby cat named 400 and a rat named Wednesday. Still her parents did not worry—until they realized that these imaginary beings were starting to control Jani. Lost in a scary world that she called Calalini, Jani was tormented by constant hallucinations. Her father, Michael Schofield, writes: "The happy, smiling girl started to fade, replaced by one who seemed angry at everything and everybody."[32] A little at a time, Jani was sinking into the terrifying depths of psychosis.

> " For a child to be stricken with schizophrenia is exceptionally rare, with estimates ranging from 1 in 30,000 to 1 in 50,000, compared with 1 in 100 adults. "

Jani's behavior turned violent when she was four and a half. She began to fly into rages, kicking her parents, hitting them with her closed fists, and biting them until she drew blood. "One minute she would be really sweet and loving and all of sudden she'd just turn," says Schofield. "Literally it was like the *Exorcist*—she would become another person. Her eyes would change, her demeanor changed, her voice flattened out. Her imaginary friends are not imaginary at all but command hallucinations. They tell her to hurt herself or someone else."[33] And Jani *did* hurt herself. During a stay at a psychiatric hospital, she bit furniture until her mouth bled because she said it made her teeth feel better. She slammed her head against the wall and tried to jump out of the window of her room. Finally, Jani was diagnosed with childhood schizophrenia—and the hospital psychiatrist said that he had never seen a case like hers in his entire 30-year career.

A Daily Struggle

Now eight years old, Jani has been fighting her terrible disease for most of her young life. She has been hospitalized numerous times and has tried a variety of antipsychotic medications. One helped for a while, but then it induced in dystonia, a disorder that causes spasms and loss of muscle control. Another seemed to ease her psychotic symptoms, but then it also caused dystonia, making her scream in terror because she could not swallow. A drug called clozapine helped her more than any other medication, diminishing her hallucinations and making her seem more like herself with no adverse side effects. But it is the most powerful antipsychotic that exists, one that carries the life-threatening risk of destroying white cells in the bloodstream.

The Schofields try to remain positive, but that is growing more and more difficult. For now, all they can do is keep giving Jani antipsychotics in doses low enough not to cause side effects, which means the drugs are not effective much of the time. But as Schofield says, they have no other choice: "Without medication, I have no doubt anymore that Jani would be dead within days, if not hours. She would continue to hurt herself until she gave herself a fatal wound. Yes, on the meds she doesn't function very well, but without them she doesn't function at all. . . . Without meds, Calalini totally dominates her existence."[34] In the absence of a cure for schizophrenia, Schofield and his wife vow to do everything in their power to keep their little girl alive, safe—and as far away from Calalini as possible.

A Heartbreaking Illness

Schizophrenia is a mystifying, frightening disorder of the brain. It can creep up on someone over time or cause the sudden onset of psychosis with no warning whatsoever. Those who suffer from it often go through years of pain, fear, and frustration before they are able to get the treatment they need—but for some, like little Jani Schofield, nothing seems to help.

66 **Schizophrenia is a severe, persistent, debilitating, and poorly understood psychiatric disorder that probably consists of several separate illnesses.** 99

—Frances R. Frankenburg, "Schizophrenia," Medscape eMedicine, May 14, 2010. http://emedicine.medscape.com.

Frankenburg is an associate professor in the Department of Psychiatry at Boston University School of Medicine.

66 **Psychosis is not violence. It is the absence of logical thought.** 99

—Michael Schofield, "Plumbers and Carpenters and Fighters," Jani's Journey, August 15, 2010. www.janisjourney.org.

Schofield is the father of Jani Schofield, an eight-year-old girl who suffers from paranoid schizophrenia.

* Editor's Note: While the definition of a primary source can be narrowly or broadly defined, for the purposes of Compact Research, a primary source consists of: 1) results of original research presented by an organization or researcher; 2) eyewitness accounts of events, personal experience, or work experience; 3) first-person editorials offering pundits' opinions; 4) government officials presenting political plans and/or policies; 5) representatives of organizations presenting testimony or policy.

❝Many of us hear voices in our heads, but usually it's our own voice acting as our [conscience] ('You really shouldn't eat that second piece of cake!'). That's not schizophrenia. And many of us believe in something that isn't true ('Life is fair.'). That's not schizophrenia either.❞

—John M. Grohol, "13 Myths of Schizophrenia," Psych Central, January 18, 2010. http://psychcentral.com.

Grohol is a psychologist, author, and founder of the Psych Central mental health Web site.

❝People with the symptoms of schizophrenia have always stood out in society as not belonging because of the extreme oddness in the way they look or act.❞

—Lynn E. DeLisi, *100 Questions and Answers About Schizophrenia: Painful Minds.* Sudbury, MA: Jones and Bartlett, 2011.

DeLisi is a psychiatry professor at New York University's Langone Medical Center and Harvard Medical School and an attending psychiatrist at the Boston Veterans Administration Healthcare System.

❝Schizophrenia is horrible. I think it's horrible for so many reasons. It's horrible because it's a disease that strikes young people just as they hit the prime of their lives.❞

—Peter R. Schofield, a participant in "All in Your Mind," ABC Australian Story, May 11, 2009. www.abc.net.au.

Schofield is executive director of Neuroscience Research Australia in New South Wales, Australia.

66 People living with schizophrenia have historically been the target of fear, stigma, discrimination and exclusion. Until recently, most individuals living with schizophrenia were confined in psychiatric hospitals or, all too often, in jails. 99

—Preston J. Garrison, introduction to *Learning About Schizophrenia*, World Federation for Mental Health, 2008. www.wfmh.org.

Garrison is secretary-general and chief executive officer of the World Federation for Mental Health.

66 People with the disorder may hear voices other people don't hear. They may believe other people are reading their minds, controlling their thoughts, or plotting to harm them. This can terrify people with the illness and make them withdrawn or extremely agitated. 99

—National Institute of Mental Health, *Schizophrenia*, 2009. www.nimh.nih.gov.

An agency of the U.S. government, the National Institute of Mental Health is the largest scientific organization in the world specializing in mental illness.

66 I was diagnosed with schizophrenia at age 24, and that was the worst night of my life. I felt a lot of fear. Fear seemed to be the dominant emotion for me. Fear of what was happening to me and fear of the world around me. 99

—Richard Schweizer, a participant in "All in Your Mind," ABC Australian Story, May 11, 2009. www.abc.net.au.

Schweizer is a schizophrenia sufferer from Australia.

What Is Schizophrenia?

- The World Health Organization states that about **24 million** people worldwide suffer from schizophrenia.

- An estimated **2.4 million** adults in the United States suffer from schizophrenia, which represents **1.1 percent** of the population over the age of 18.

- The Schizophrenia and Related Disorders Alliance of America states that there are more Americans with schizophrenia than there are residents of **North Dakota, South Dakota, and Wyoming combined**.

- According to a 2008 survey by the National Alliance on Mental Illness, only **24 percent** of the general public consider themselves to be familiar with schizophrenia.

- The National Alliance on Mental Illness states that about **three-fourths** of people with schizophrenia develop it between the ages of 16 and 25.

- A major study published in the *British Journal of Psychiatry* in 2006 stated that the onset of psychosis is sudden (with no prodromal period) in **22.2 percent** of schizophrenia patients, occurs in less than a month in **26.7 percent** of patients, and takes longer than a month in **51.1 percent** of patients.

- According to a 2008 survey by the National Alliance on Mental Illness, **64 percent** of respondents had the erroneous perception that split or multiple personalities are symptoms of schizophrenia.

Schizophrenia in the United States

According to the National Institute of Mental Health, approximately 2.4 million American adults, or about 1.1 percent of the adult population, suffer from schizophrenia. This graph shows how its prevalence compares with that of other mental illnesses.

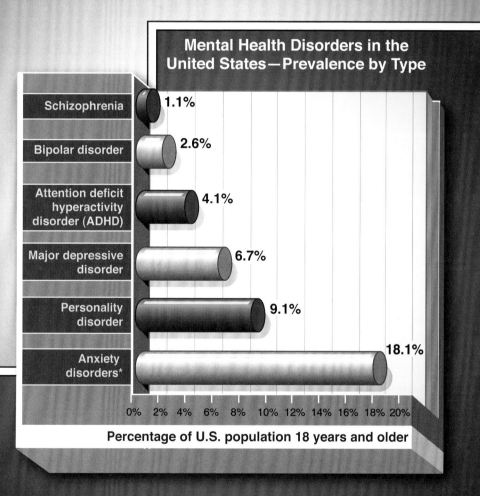

Mental Health Disorders in the United States—Prevalence by Type

Disorder	Percentage
Schizophrenia	1.1%
Bipolar disorder	2.6%
Attention deficit hyperactivity disorder (ADHD)	4.1%
Major depressive disorder	6.7%
Personality disorder	9.1%
Anxiety disorders*	18.1%

0% 2% 4% 6% 8% 10% 12% 14% 16% 18% 20%

Percentage of U.S. population 18 years and older

* Included in anxiety disorders are panic disorder, OCD, PTSD, GAD, social phobia, and specific phobia.

Source: National Institute of Mental Health, "The Numbers Count: Mental Disorders in America," July 21, 2010. www.nimh.nih.gov.

Schizophrenia

Symptoms of Schizophrenia

People who suffer from schizophrenia exhibit a number of different symptoms that mental health professionals categorize as positive, negative, or cognitive. In the context of schizophrenia, positive symptoms reflect an excess or distortion of normal functions, negative symptoms refer to the absence of characteristics of normal function, and cognitive symptoms involve problems with thought processes. This table shows the various symptoms and their characteristics.

Positive Symptoms
Delusions: Beliefs/perceptions that are not based in reality; the most common of all schizophrenia symptoms
Hallucinations: Seeing or hearing things that do not exist; most common is auditory hallucinations (hearing voices)
Thought disorder: Difficulty organizing thoughts leads to jumbled, incoherent speech or stringing together meaningless phrases ("word salad")
Disorganized behavior: May range from childlike silliness to unpredictable agitation

Negative Symptoms
Loss of interest in everyday activities
Appearing to lack emotion or feelings (flat affect)
Reduced ability to plan or carry out activities
Social withdrawal
Loss of overall motivation
Neglect of personal hygiene

Cognitive Symptoms
Problems with thought processes; inability to make sense of information
Difficulty paying attention
Memory problems

Source: Mayo Clinic, "Schizophrenia," January 30, 2010. www.mayoclinic.com.

Low Public Awareness of Schizophrenia

In a February 2008 survey commissioned by the National Alliance on Mental Illness, 1,012 participants in the general public were asked how familiar they were with mental health disorders and certain diseases. As this graph illustrates, schizophrenia is one of the least understood.

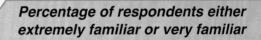

Percentage of respondents either extremely familiar or very familiar

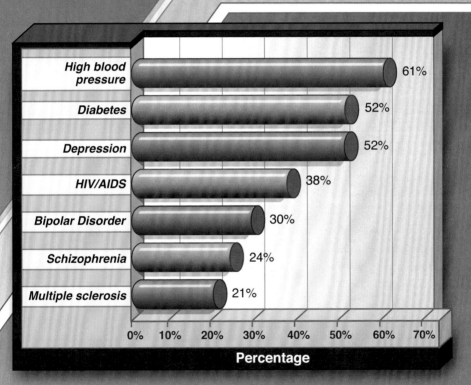

Disorder	Percentage
High blood pressure	61%
Diabetes	52%
Depression	52%
HIV/AIDS	38%
Bipolar Disorder	30%
Schizophrenia	24%
Multiple sclerosis	21%

Percentage

Source: National Alliance on Mental Illness, *Schizophrenia: Public Attitudes, Personal Needs*, April 25, 2008. www.nami.org.

- Patients with a mental illness known as **schizophreniform disorder** have many or all of the symptoms of schizophrenia, but these resolve themselves within six months without any residual effects.

- According to the National Institute of Mental Health, a combination of factors (withdrawal and isolation, an increase in unusual thoughts and suspicions, and a family history of psychosis) can predict schizophrenia in **80 percent** of youth who are at high risk of developing the disease.

- Schizophrenia is estimated to affect between **1 in 30,000** and **1 in 50,000 children**, compared with **1 in 100 adults**.

- The National Alliance on Mental Illness states that the economic cost of untreated mental illness is more than **$100 billion** each year in the United States.

- According to neurologist Nitin Gogtay, **child-onset schizophrenia** is 20 to 30 times more severe than adult-onset schizophrenia.

What Causes Schizophrenia?

> **❝It's not known what causes schizophrenia, but researchers believe that a combination of genetics and environment contributes to development of the disease.❞**
>
> —Mayo Clinic, a world-renowned medical facility headquartered in Rochester, Minnesota.

> **❝Recent research has found that people with schizophrenia tend to have higher rates of rare genetic mutations. These genetic differences involve hundreds of different genes and probably disrupt brain development.❞**
>
> —National Institute of Mental Health, the largest scientific organization in the world specializing in mental illness.

Scientists and physicians have long speculated about the cause of schizophrenia. Widely diverse theories have been proposed over the years, ranging from demonic possession and other supernatural causes to bacterial infection and dysfunctional family environment. The role of family was a topic of immense interest during the mid-twentieth century, with a theory posited by Frieda Fromm-Reichmann, a well-known German psychiatrist. In 1948 Fromm-Reichmann published a paper in which she attributed the development of schizophrenia to cold, aloof, hostile mothers. She wrote: "The schizophrenic is painfully distrustful and resentful of other people due to the severe early warp and rejection he encountered in important people of his infancy and childhood, as a rule, mainly a schizophrenogenic mother."[35]

Fromm-Reichmann coined the derogatory term *schizophrenogenic mother*, and her theory was embraced by many of her peers—but it has long since been debunked. Scientists now know that schizophrenia is a disease of the brain and that it is *not* caused by parental behavior toward children. While stress, including within a family environment, may trigger the onset of psychotic symptoms, schizophrenia can only develop if the person is already biologically vulnerable to it.

The Incredible Brain

Perhaps one of the greatest unknowns of medical science is why the brains of people with schizophrenia are different from those who do not have the disease. A number of differences have been confirmed through magnetic resonance imaging (MRI) scans, but there are still more questions than answers. Thus, a great deal of scientific research has focused on the brain—specifically, how it works and the various functions it performs.

The human brain is the most complicated living structure that is known to exist. It controls humans' ability to see, smell, taste, hear, speak, feel, learn, remember, and respond to the world around them. The National Institute of Neurological Disorders and Stroke explains: "The brain is the most complex part of the human body. This three-pound organ is the seat of intelligence, interpreter of the senses, initiator of body movement, and controller of behavior. Lying in its bony shell and washed by protective fluid, the brain is the source of all the qualities that define our humanity. The brain is the crown jewel of the human body."[36]

> " Fromm-Reichmann coined the derogatory term *schizophrenogenic mother*, and her theory was embraced by many of her peers—but it has long since been debunked. "

The brain is composed of different types of cells, but at the heart of its immense power is a complex network of cells known as neurons. Like a rapid-fire version of instant messaging on Facebook, neurons constantly transmit messages to and from each other, and to various organs in the body, in the form of electrical signals. In the process, neurons release chemicals called neurotransmitters into synapses, the tiny gaps between neurons. The function of neurotransmitters is to assist in transferring information from one neuron to another across synapses. Dean A. Haycock writes: "This process is conducted continuously, even while you sleep, on an unimaginably vast scale, involving billions of brain cells. In ways we don't understand, it helps the brain produce consciousness, dreams, thoughts, feelings, and emotions. When the mechanism malfunctions, the result can be hallucinations, paranoia, depression, and other symptoms of mental illness."[37]

The Brain's Balancing Act

Neurotransmitters serve as mechanisms that either excite or inhibit the brain, with some performing both functions. The role of those in the excitatory category is to provide energy, motivation, and other activities that require action of the brain and body. Inhibitory neurotransmitters perform in the opposite way, having a calming effect on the mind and body by inducing sleep and filtering out unnecessary excitatory signals. Neurotransmitters working together in this way result in a meticulously coordinated effort that is crucial for the brain to work correctly.

As mental health therapist Sheryl Ankrom writes: "For optimal brain function, neurotransmitters must be carefully balanced and orchestrated. They are often interconnected and rely on each other for proper function."[38]

> When neurotransmitters are out of balance, this can wreak havoc on the brain's ability to function.

When neurotransmitters are out of balance, this can wreak havoc on the brain's ability to function. For instance, dopamine (which performs both inhibitory and excitatory tasks) helps regulate mood, feelings of pleasure, thoughts, and motivation. If dopamine levels are abnormally high—which they typically are in schizophrenia patients—this can lead to psychotic behaviors. Because of that, the potential link between schizophrenia and excessive amounts of dopamine has been of interest to scientists for years. Much still remains unknown, however, as Heather Barnett Veague, the clinical research director for Vassar College's Laboratory of Adolescent Sciences, explains: "We still don't know what causes this excess of dopamine. Do some people produce too much dopamine? Is the breakdown of dopamine somehow inhibited in some people? Or do some people have dopamine receptors that are especially sensitive so their brain thinks that there is extra dopamine even when there isn't? These are questions that have yet to be answered definitively."[39]

Glutamate is another neurotransmitter that has been implicated in the development of schizophrenia. Studies have shown that too much glutamate in the brain can cause neurons to die, as well as cause seizures, while insufficient levels can result in delusions, hallucinations, and cognitive difficulties. Scientists are interested in exploring this further to understand glutamate better, including how it works together with dopamine in the brain. Some researchers theorize that the interaction between these two neurotransmitters could play a major role in schizophrenia.

Clues Within Children's Brains

Because childhood schizophrenia causes such severe psychosis in children, studying it is a high priority for scientists. In October 2008 researchers from the National Institute of Mental Health made a discovery that could lead to better understanding of the disease—and perhaps serve as a stepping-stone toward prevention. Over a period of 5 years, the team used MRI technology to scan the brains of 12 children with schizophrenia, as well as 12 healthy children. By superimposing one scan onto another as the children grew, the researchers could gauge how fast the different areas of their brains were growing.

> "
> Scientists generally agree that schizophrenia results from a complex interaction between heredity and living environment.
> "

In analyzing the children's brain scans, the team could see significant differences in the white matter in the children's brains. Whereas gray matter is composed of densely packed neurons, white matter is made up of nerve fibers, and it fills nearly half of the human brain. A March 2008 *Scientific American* article explains how crucial this is: "White matter is composed of millions of communications cables, each one containing a long, individual wire, or axon, coated with a white, fatty substance called myelin. Like the trunk lines that connect telephones in different parts of a country, this white cabling connects neurons in one region of the brain with those in other regions."[40]

The National Institute of Mental Health researchers found that in the children with schizophrenia, white matter was growing 2.2 percent more slowly per year than normal on the right side of the brain. On the left side, growth of white matter was only 1.3 percent per year, compared with 2.6 percent yearly growth in the healthy children. This was an important finding because the slower the rate of growth, the worse the outcome for children with schizophrenia. The

> "
> **Numerous studies have shown a link between mothers who were exposed to the influenza virus while they were pregnant and development of schizophrenia in their offspring later in life.**
> "

researchers hope that further use of MRI technology can eventually lead to better diagnostic techniques to enable treatments to be started earlier.

The Genetic Connection

Research has repeatedly shown that schizophrenia runs in families. There are, however, many unanswered questions about the hereditary nature of the disease. Haycock writes:

> There are undeniably strong links between the genes a person is born with and her risk of developing schizophrenia, yet the connection is not absolute. If one of your relatives has schizophrenia, it does not mean you will have schizophrenia. It only means that you may have a slightly greater chance than the average person of developing the disease. That depends on how closely you are related to the person with schizophrenia.[41]

When both parents have schizophrenia, their children have about a 45 percent chance of developing it. With identical twins, if one twin has schizophrenia, the chances range from 40 to 65 percent that the other will develop the disease.

Even though research has proved that genetics plays a major role in the development of schizophrenia, genes alone do not cause the disease. This becomes obvious when considering that most people who are genetically predisposed to the disease never go on to develop it. Scientists generally agree that schizophrenia results from a complex interaction between heredity and living environment. New York psychiatrists Cheryl Corcoran and Dolores Malaspina refer to this as the "two-hit" hypothesis of schizophrenia: "that genetic vulnerability or problems in the womb set the stage for schizophrenia, but that a second event in adolescence or early adulthood leads to the development of schizophrenia. This 'second hit' may be a major life event or episode of stress."[42]

The Vulnerable Fetus

Corcoran and Malaspina's reference to "problems in the womb" is a topic of immense interest to researchers who are studying schizophrenia. The time that a fetus spends growing and developing inside its mother is crucial because major organs—especially the brain—are highly vulnerable to damage during the development phase.

Viruses have been identified as one of the major potential risk factors for schizophrenia. For instance, numerous studies have shown a link between mothers who were exposed to the influenza virus while they were pregnant and development of schizophrenia in their offspring later in life. Stuart C. Yudofsky, who is a psychiatrist at the Baylor College of Medicine in Houston, Texas, writes:

> Although this idea has been debated in the scientific literature, many studies have documented that schizophrenia occurs more frequently in children born in winter and early spring when viral infections are more prevalent. Among 25 investigations of the incidence of schizophrenia in the offspring of women who were thought to have contracted influenza during pregnancy, approximately 50% reported positive associations.[43]

A study published in March 2010 further strengthened the connection between the flu virus and schizophrenia. Researchers from North Carolina and Wisconsin performed experiments with rhesus monkeys, infecting 12 of them with a mild influenza virus a month before their babies were due. For comparison purposes, 7 other pregnant monkeys were not infected with the virus. The team observed the babies of flu-infected mothers for months after they were born and saw no physical or behavioral effects related to influenza. When the babies were 1 year old (the equivalent of 5 to 7 years in humans), MRI scans were taken of their brains. The scans revealed that the brains of the young flu-exposed monkeys were significantly smaller than those of the monkeys whose mothers were not infected with influenza.

This was an important finding because of what it could mean for schizophrenia in the offspring of flu-infected pregnant women. John H. Gilmore, a University of North Carolina psychiatry professor and one of the researchers involved in the study, explains:

> The brain changes that we found in the monkey babies are similar to what we typically see in MRI scans of humans with schizophrenia. This suggests that human babies whose mothers had the flu while pregnant may have a greater risk of developing schizophrenia later in life than babies whose mothers did not have the flu. Normally that risk affects about 1 of every 100 births. Studies in humans suggest that for flu-exposed babies, the risk is 2 or 3 per 100 births.[44]

This sort of research can help scientists gain a better understanding of how viruses contribute to schizophrenia. It may also lead to efforts such as widespread influenza vaccination for all women of childbearing age, which could potentially prevent some types of schizophrenia.

Lingering Questions

A wealth of information about schizophrenia has been gained since the 1940s, when the disease was erroneously (and unfairly) blamed on mothers. Scientists now know that schizophrenia originates in the brain, and research has provided a number of potential contributing factors such as an imbalance of neurotransmitters and exposure to the influenza virus. Yet there is so much more that remains to be discovered about schizophrenia and its causes. As research continues, more answers will undoubtedly be revealed.

Primary Source Quotes*

What Causes Schizophrenia?

66 **Multiple studies indicate that pregnant women who get influenza during the first half of their pregnancy give birth to children who are more likely to develop schizophrenia than children whose mothers did not suffer from the flu.** 99

—Dean A. Haycock, *The Everything Health Guide to Schizophrenia*. Avon, MA: Adams Media, 2009.

Haycock is a science and medical writer who holds a PhD in neuroscience.

....

66 **One of the more prevalent theories about these viruses is that a mother acquires the infection during her second trimester of pregnancy . . . making offspring more vulnerable to develop schizophrenia in later life. This is just a theory for which there is not yet convincing substantiating evidence.** 99

—Lynn E. DeLisi, *100 Questions and Answers About Schizophrenia: Painful Minds*. Sudbury, MA: Jones and Bartlett, 2011.

DeLisi is a psychiatry professor at New York University's Langone Medical Center and Harvard Medical School and an attending psychiatrist at the Boston Veterans Administration Healthcare System.

....

* Editor's Note: While the definition of a primary source can be narrowly or broadly defined, for the purposes of Compact Research, a primary source consists of: 1) results of original research presented by an organization or researcher; 2) eyewitness accounts of events, personal experience, or work experience; 3) first-person editorials offering pundits' opinions; 4) government officials presenting political plans and/or policies; 5) representatives of organizations presenting testimony or policy.

Primary Source Quotes

" If no one in the immediate biological family of first degree relatives has schizophrenia or a related condition, that is a good sign. Multiple relatives who share schizophrenia outcomes is a bad sign. "

—Rashmi Nemade and Mark Dombeck, "An Introduction to Schizophrenia and Schizoaffective Disorders," Mental Help Net, August 7, 2009. www.mentalhelp.net.

Nemade and Dombeck are psychologists and contributors to the Mental Help Net Web site.

" Women who are malnourished or who have certain viral illnesses during their pregnancy may be at greater risk of giving birth to children who later develop schizophrenia. "

—Frances R. Frankenburg, "Schizophrenia," Medscape eMedicine, May 14, 2010. http://emedicine.medscape.com.

Frankenburg is an associate professor in the Department of Psychiatry at Boston University School of Medicine.

" There is no evidence that family relationships cause schizophrenia, but if there is tension in the family, people with schizophrenia seem very sensitive to the tension, and this sensitivity to tension may be the 'trigger' that sets off an episode of illness. "

—Children, Youth, and Women's Health Service, "Schizophrenia," May 13, 2010. www.cyh.com.

Based in South Australia, the Children, Youth, and Women's Health Service is dedicated to the health and well-being of young people and their families.

" Children with fathers who are over the age of 50 are three times more likely to develop schizophrenia than children whose fathers are under 30 years old at the time of their birth. "

—Jerome Levine and Irene S. Levine, *Schizophrenia for Dummies*. Hoboken, NJ: Wiley, 2009.

The Levines are professors of psychiatry at the New York University School of Medicine.

66 **Marijuana has indisputably been shown to increase the risk for schizophrenia. Kids, when they smoke marijuana during adolescence, are doubling, tripling, or quadrupling their chances of developing schizophrenia.** 99

—Jeffrey Lieberman, "Is Schizophrenia Preventable?" EmpowHER, August 17, 2009. www.empowher.com.

Lieberman is chair of the Department of Psychiatry at the Columbia University College of Physicians and Surgeons, director of the New York State Psychiatric Institute, and director of the Lieber Center for Schizophrenia Research.

66 **Schizophrenia may also be triggered by environmental events, such as viral infections or highly stressful situations or a combination of both.** 99

—Mental Health America, "Factsheet: Schizophrenia; What You Need to Know," 2010. www.nmha.org.

Mental Health America is dedicated to helping people live mentally healthier lives and to educating the public about mental health and mental illness.

What Causes Schizophrenia?

- The National Institute of Mental Health states that schizophrenia affects **10 percent** of people who have an immediate family member with the disorder.

- Although schizophrenia has been shown to be hereditary, an estimated **60 percent** of people who develop it do not have a close family member with the disease.

- **Magnetic resonance imaging** scans have shown a number of abnormalities in the brain's structure that have been associated with schizophrenia.

- According to psychiatrist Stuart C. Yudofsky, among 25 investigations of women who contracted influenza during pregnancy, **50 percent** of their offspring developed schizophrenia.

- According to the National Institute of Mental Health, research has found strong evidence of a link between **marijuana use and schizophrenia symptoms**.

- Studies have shown that the risk for schizophrenia worldwide is **5 to 8 percent** higher for babies that are born in winter and spring than during summer and fall.

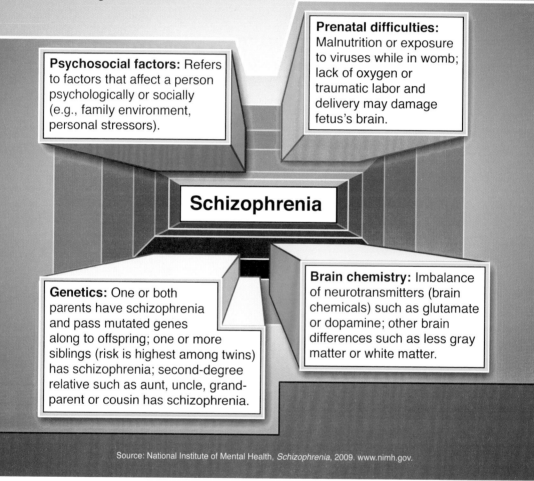

Biology and Environment

Scientists believe that schizophrenia develops due to the interaction of different factors such as genetics, brain chemistry, environment, and prenatal difficulties. This illustration shows how such factors may work together to cause the disease.

Prenatal difficulties: Malnutrition or exposure to viruses while in womb; lack of oxygen or traumatic labor and delivery may damage fetus's brain.

Psychosocial factors: Refers to factors that affect a person psychologically or socially (e.g., family environment, personal stressors).

Schizophrenia

Genetics: One or both parents have schizophrenia and pass mutated genes along to offspring; one or more siblings (risk is highest among twins) has schizophrenia; second-degree relative such as aunt, uncle, grandparent or cousin has schizophrenia.

Brain chemistry: Imbalance of neurotransmitters (brain chemicals) such as glutamate or dopamine; other brain differences such as less gray matter or white matter.

Source: National Institute of Mental Health, *Schizophrenia*, 2009. www.nimh.gov.

- In experiments with mice, researchers from the University of Minnesota Medical School found a direct connection between **H1N1 influenza infection in pregnant females** and the onset of autism, schizophrenia, and other brain disorders in their offspring.

Stunted Brain Growth in Children with Schizophrenia

Although scientists do not know why it occurs, research has shown that the brains of people with schizophrenia are different from those who do not have the disease. In a study announced in October 2008, research from the National Institute of Mental Health found that white matter (indicated in maroon) in the brains of children with schizophrenia was growing at a much slower rate than in the brains of healthy children. These illustrations depict brain scans showing the differences between the two groups.

Healthy Children

Males & Females

Children with Schizophrenia

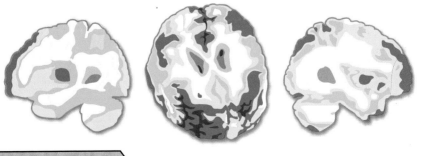

Males & Females

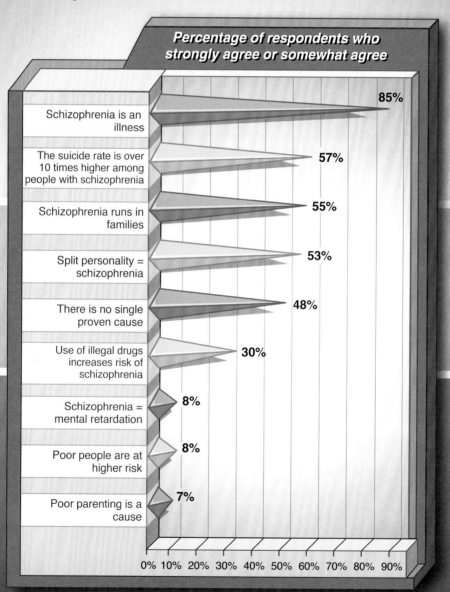

Public Perception of Schizophrenia

In a February 2008 survey for the National Alliance on Mental Illness, members of the general population were asked to share their views on a number of statements about schizophrenia, including its causes.

Percentage of respondents who strongly agree or somewhat agree

Statement	Percentage
Schizophrenia is an illness	85%
The suicide rate is over 10 times higher among people with schizophrenia	57%
Schizophrenia runs in families	55%
Split personality = schizophrenia	53%
There is no single proven cause	48%
Use of illegal drugs increases risk of schizophrenia	30%
Schizophrenia = mental retardation	8%
Poor people are at higher risk	8%
Poor parenting is a cause	7%

0% 10% 20% 30% 40% 50% 60% 70% 80% 90%

Source: National Alliance on Mental Illness, *Schizophrenia: Public Attitudes, Personal Needs*, April 25, 2008. www.nami.org.

- According to psychologists Rashmi Nemade and Mark Dombeck, female vulnerability to schizophrenia peaks twice: first between **25 and 30** years, then again around **40** years of age.

- The World Federation for Mental Health states that although stress does not cause schizophrenia, it has been proved that **stress makes symptoms worse** when the illness is already present.

- Studies have suggested that children born to fathers over the age of 50 are **2 to 3 times more likely** to develop schizophrenia than children whose fathers were under 30 years old at the time of their birth.

- A major study conducted by researchers in Finland found that people who were genetically vulnerable to developing schizophrenia were especially sensitive to the **emotional climate of their family environment**.

What Problems Are Associated with Schizophrenia?

66Teen years are difficult enough without the added burden of schizophrenia. . . . Left untreated normal development will suffer, school performance will diminish, anti-social activities may increase, depression and suicidal thoughts and behavior may become evident.99

> —Jerry Kennard, a psychologist who is an associate fellow and chartered member of the British Psychological Society.

66Schizophrenia is a severe and debilitating disorder, which affects general health, functioning, autonomy, subjective well being, and life satisfaction of those who suffer from it.99

> —Ram Kumar Solanki, Paramjeet Singh, Aarti Midha, and Karan Chugh, psychiatrists from India.

A Florida woman named Jennifer is painfully familiar with the suffering caused by schizophrenia. She was not affected by it until she was in her twenties and suddenly found herself overcome with psychotic thoughts. She writes:

> I started to think paranoid things about people being after me, the CIA tracking me . . . my thoughts being controlled by the government and other bizarre beliefs.

I began to see the same colors everywhere, such as red, white, and blue everywhere I went. I began to think I was being followed at all times, by various people. I saw things which I did not realize until some years later, had been hallucinations.[45]

Jennifer's condition continued to worsen until she was deep in the throes of psychosis. "I began hearing voices," she says. "I also thought I was being communicated with directly by people on television and the radio. I thought that people could read my mind, and that I could read others' minds. I did not associate these symptoms with having a mental illness because, at the time, I did not possess that kind of insight."[46]

Eventually Jennifer got psychiatric help and started taking medications that eased her symptoms and helped quiet the voices. Today she is no longer a prisoner to the delusions and hallucinations that used to haunt her day and night. Yet even though her life is a vast improvement over what it was, all is not well in Jennifer's world. She often gets despondent,

> **One of the worst problems for many people with schizophrenia is the difficulty of maintaining personal relationships. Their illness often causes them to become withdrawn and isolated, even from family and friends.**

as she explains: "I am discouraged by how long it has taken me to get to the point that I am at. I have a hard time feeling like anything I do is worthwhile. I get discouraged. I get depressed. I lose hope."[47]

Because of all that she has been though, and the feelings of failure and inadequacy that she cannot push away, Jennifer sometimes gets wistful about the past. She cannot help but long for the time when she knew nothing whatsoever about living with schizophrenia:

Actually I miss that a lot. I miss being one of those people who thought Schizophrenia was related to being a serial killer and not something that would ever happen to a nice girl like me. I miss that ignorance, which, as they say, was bliss. I miss believing that I would be able to do all those things that people expected me to be able to do, because I was intelligent enough to do them, and because I wasn't psychotic then. . . . I wish I could be that young woman again, so full of promise, hope, and owning such a future that I can only visit in my dreams now.[48]

Solitary Suffering

One of the worst problems for many people with schizophrenia is the difficulty of maintaining personal relationships. Their illness often causes them to become withdrawn and isolated, even from family and friends. Dean A. Haycock writes: "Hallucinations, delusions, and bizarre behavior turn people inward. It is impossible to focus on routine tasks and social interactions when you are dealing with voices that comment on your every action, or when you are living with the knowledge that special messages just for you are being broadcast on the news or hidden in street signs." Haycock adds that the bizarre behaviors exhibited by someone with schizophrenia can strain existing relationships and prevent people from creating new ones. "The average person does not make an effort to establish or even maintain a casual or intimate relationship with someone struggling with severe mental illness. Consequently, people struggling with psychosis often lose established relationships, and more than half never marry."[49]

> " One thing that is especially hurtful for many with schizophrenia is the erroneous belief that everyone who suffers from it is violent and dangerous. "

Another difficult challenge for those with schizophrenia is the negativity they encounter from society. Often this is because their hallucinations, disorganized thinking, and other psychotic behaviors can be frightening to people who encounter them. Sathnam Sanghera, whose father and sister have schizophrenia, shares his thoughts: "I have been struck by how commonly friends and family members abandon sufferers because the symptoms—which can include hearing voices, feeling that your thoughts are being broadcast to the outside world, feeling that things are crawling beneath the skin, and believing an alien force is directing you—are so terrifying that people don't know what to do and end up running away." Sanghera agrees that sufferers are not treated very well by society, as he writes: "Schizophrenia really is the modern equivalent of leprosy. I have counselled friends through depression and, as shattering as the effects have been on them, they do not compare to what schizophrenia has done to my family."[50]

A Child's Living Nightmare

Mental health professionals often say that when schizophrenia strikes children, their suffering is much more severe than that of adults. This can have a profound impact on their young lives, as Judith Rapoport explains: "I think this is a very taxing, a very stressful condition for the child to have. The children are aware that they've lost many of their abilities. . . . It's not just that the voices interfere, but there's something about the process that does make it harder for them to think and concentrate." Rapoport adds that having to cope with schizophrenia can make youngsters feel depressed and alone: "The children are very sad. They see that they don't have friends, and that they're different and not all of them, but many of them, are actually very aware of what they are losing by having this disorder."[51]

Rebecca Stancil has endured more than her share of suffering for a child who is just 10 years old. Diagnosed with paranoid schizophrenia, Rebecca has suffered from hallucinations since she was three, including ominous shadows and shapes that skulk around darkened rooms. One of her most frightening—and relentless—hallucinations is a larger-than-life man with a monster's face who Rebecca says watches her constantly and follows her everywhere. Her mother, Cinnamon Stancil, explains: "She sees him, and he's putting a gun to her head telling her she has to run away. She got to the point where she wanted to run away, run on the freeway and get hit by a car to stop the man from coming."[52]

Even at her young age, Rebecca has tried to kill herself in a desperate attempt to get rid of the visions and voices that constantly haunt her. On more than one occasion, she has also tried to kill her mother. Rebecca has gone after her with knives and most any other object she can find, such as the heavy lid from the back of the toilet. She once ripped wires out of the video game system and headed toward her mother, intending to choke her. Of course Cinnamon knows that Rebecca's illness is to blame for her violent behavior, and Rebecca knows it too—but that cannot erase the horror she is forced to endure every day. During a news program, a journalist asked Rebecca what it was like to be her. She became visibly agitated, and the answer she gave in a voice that was part anger and part anguish revealed a glimpse into a little girl's tortured mind: "I hate being Rebecca. I hate it, I hate it."[53]

The Violence Controversy

One thing that is especially hurtful for many with schizophrenia is the erroneous belief that everyone who suffers from it is violent and dangerous. In a June 2008 survey by the National Alliance on Mental Illness, 60 percent of participants listed violent behavior as a symptom of the disease. As much as the National Alliance on Mental Illness and other mental health organizations try to dispel this notion through education and awareness efforts, violence and schizophrenia remain intertwined in many people's minds. Elyn R. Saks has encountered that perception many times during her struggle with schizophrenia. In reference to a schizophrenia sufferer who stabbed his pregnant wife to death, Saks writes: "The media frenzy that surrounded it only added to the mythology that fuels the stigma: that schizophrenics are violent and threatening. In truth, the large majority of schizophrenics never harm anyone; in fact, if and when they do, they're far more likely to harm themselves than anyone else."[54]

> Some research has shown that schizophrenia sufferers *are* more likely to commit violent acts.

Most mental health professionals agree that people with schizophrenia pose a greater risk to themselves than to others, but whether they are more prone to violence is a topic of much debate. Some research has shown that schizophrenia sufferers *are* more likely to commit violent acts. One study was led by Seena Fazel, a psychiatrist from the United Kingdom, and was published in August 2009. Fazel and his colleagues examined 20 different studies that focused on the connection between schizophrenia (and other psychotic disorders) and violence. More than 18,000 people with psychosis were analyzed along with a control group of 1.7 million healthy people. The researchers found that 9.9 percent of those with psychosis had committed violent crimes, compared with 1.6 percent in the general population.

Another finding of the study was that people with psychotic disorders were significantly more inclined to be violent if they abused alcohol or drugs. This is a common problem among people with schizophrenia, as the National Institute of Mental Health explains: "People who have schizophrenia are much more likely to have a substance or alcohol abuse problem than the general population. . . . Some drugs, like marijuana and stimulants such as amphetamines or cocaine, may make symptoms worse. In fact, research has found increasing evidence of a link between marijuana and schizophrenia symptoms."[55] According to Fazel's study, those with psychotic illnesses who abused alcohol and/or drugs were four times more likely to commit violent acts than the people who suffered with psychosis only.

> **According to the National Institute of Mental Health, smoking is a major problem among schizophrenia sufferers, with nicotine being the most common form of substance abuse.**

The Cancer Risk

Scientists have long known that many people with schizophrenia suffer from serious health problems such as substance abuse, obesity, and diabetes. A study announced in June 2009 showed that they also have a heightened risk of cancer. A team of researchers from France, led by psychiatrist Frederic Limosin, found that schizophrenia patients were 50 percent more likely to die from cancer than the general population and that cancer was their second most common cause of death after suicide. The study was conducted over a period of 11 years. It involved 3,470 people with schizophrenia, of whom 476 (13.7 percent) died—a mortality rate 4 times higher than the general population. Of those deaths, 30 percent of the patients died from suicide and 15.5 percent died from cancer.

Another finding was that the proportion of patients who were smokers was significantly high: 56.3 percent compared with 33 percent in the general population. According to the National Institute of Mental Health, smoking is a major problem among schizophrenia sufferers, with nicotine being the most common form of substance abuse. The group adds that people with schizophrenia are addicted to nicotine at three times the rate of the general population. In reference to Limosin's study, it is probable that there was a strong connection between the large percentage of smokers and the high number of cancer deaths. Limosin explains: "Our results emphasize the necessity for psychiatrists, but also general practitioners, to assess risk factors of cancer in schizophrenic patients (especially smoking) and to detect cancer occurrence as early as possible."[56]

A Painful Way to Live

People with schizophrenia endure a multitude of problems because of their illness. From children terrorized by ominous shadows and evil beings to adult sufferers having to face stigmas imposed by society, life is far from easy. Sanghera has seen firsthand how difficult living with schizophrenia can be for those who suffer from it, as he writes:

> My father is a gentle and kind man and has been stable for a long time. But he had to live through decades of violent breakdowns, suicidal episodes, a period of imprisonment, endless firings from jobs due to erratic behaviour, and unexplained domestic violence before he got there. And this is what accounts of family lives blighted by schizophrenia are like: the painful narrative keeps lurching forward bleakly until the medication starts working or someone—usually the sufferer—dies.[57]

Primary Source Quotes*

What Problems Are Associated with Schizophrenia?

66 **The vast majority of people with schizophrenia are *not* violent and do not pose a danger to others.** 99

—Mental Health America, "Factsheet: Schizophrenia; What You Need to Know," 2010. www.nmha.org.

Mental Health America is dedicated to helping people live mentally healthier lives and to educating the public about mental health and mental illness.

66 **Schizophrenia increases the risk of violence by six to 10-fold in men and eight to 10-fold in women.** 99

—Stéphane Richard-Devantoy, Jean-Pierre Olie, and Raphaël Gourévitch, "Risk of Homicide and Major Mental Disorders: A Critical Review," *Encephale*, December 2009. www.ncbi.nlm.nih.gov.

Richard-Devantoy, Olie, and Gourévitch are psychiatrists from France.

* Editor's Note: While the definition of a primary source can be narrowly or broadly defined, for the purposes of Compact Research, a primary source consists of: 1) results of original research presented by an organization or researcher; 2) eyewitness accounts of events, personal experience, or work experience; 3) first-person editorials offering pundits' opinions; 4) government officials presenting political plans and/or policies; 5) representatives of organizations presenting testimony or policy.

Primary Source Quotes

❝What happens to people with schizophrenia varies greatly according to sex, age at its onset, the speed of onset, awareness of the illness and initial response to medication. But basically it is a lifelong condition with no cure.❞

—Sathnam Sanghera, "Schizophrenia Is the Modern Leprosy," *Sunday Times*, February 5, 2009. www.timesonline.co.uk.

Sanghera is a writer from the United Kingdom whose father and sister suffer from schizophrenia.

❝People living with schizophrenia die from heart disease, diabetes, and other medical causes at a rate two or three times greater than the rest of the population.❞

—National Alliance on Mental Illness, *Schizophrenia: Public Attitudes, Personal Needs.* June 10, 2008. www.nami.org.

The National Alliance on Mental Illness is dedicated to improving the lives of people who are affected by mental illness, as well as the lives of their families.

❝Schizophrenia doesn't directly kill you, like, let's say, cancer will kill you or Alzheimer's disease will result in mortality, but it indirectly has a high mortality rate.❞

—Jeffrey Lieberman, "Is Schizophrenia a Fatal Diagnosis?" EmpowHER, April 17, 2009. www.empowher.com.

Lieberman is chair of the Department of Psychiatry at the Columbia University College of Physicians and Surgeons, director of the New York State Psychiatric Institute, and director of the Lieber Center for Schizophrenia Research.

❝A particularly difficult issue can arise for families because some people with schizophrenia do not realise or accept that they are unwell—this is generally considered to be a symptom of the illness and is called 'lack of insight.'❞

—World Federation for Mental Health, *Learning About Schizophrenia*, 2008. www.wfmh.org.

The World Federation for Mental Health is dedicated to the prevention of mental and emotional disorders, proper care and treatment for those with such disorders, and promotion of mental health.

❝More than one half of children with schizophrenia have persistent severe impairment in social skills and limitations in academic and occupational achievement.❞

—Raj K. Kalapatapu and David W. Dunn, "Schizophrenia and Other Psychoses," Medscape eMedicine, May 26, 2010. http://emedicine.medscape.com.

Kalapatapu is a fellow in addiction psychiatry at the Columbia University College of Physicians and Surgeons, and Dunn is program director in the Department of Child and Adolescent Psychiatry at Indiana University.

❝Sometimes symptoms become severe for people who stop their medication and treatment. This is dangerous, since they may become unable to care for themselves. Some people end up on the street or in jail, where they rarely receive the kind of help they need.❞

——National Institute of Mental Health, *Schizophrenia*, 2009. www.nimh.nih.gov.

An agency of the U.S. government, the National Institute of Mental Health is the largest scientific organization in the world specializing in mental illness.

What Problems Are Associated with Schizophrenia?

- The World Health Organization has identified schizophrenia as one of the **10 most debilitating diseases affecting people worldwide**.

- According to Boston psychiatrist Frances R. Frankenburg, **20 to 70 percent** of people with schizophrenia also have a substance abuse problem.

- The World Federation for Mental Health states that compared with the general population, people with schizophrenia have higher rates of **dental disease, diabetes, cardiovascular diseases, respiratory disease, hepatitis C, and HIV**.

- A comprehensive study published in 2009 by researchers from the United Kingdom and Sweden found that **9.9 percent** of people with schizophrenia and other psychotic illnesses had committed violent crimes, compared with **1.6 percent** of the general population.

- According to the Schizophrenia and Related Disorders Alliance of America, between **33 percent** and **50 percent** of all homeless adults have schizophrenia.

- In a 2008 survey by the National Alliance on Mental Illness, **27 percent** of respondents said they would be embarrassed to tell others if one of their family members was diagnosed with schizophrenia.

Reactions Toward Schizophrenics

People with schizophrenia encounter a number of different reactions—both negative and positive—when others find out about their illnesses. This graph shows experiences that were shared by schizophrenia sufferers during a February 2008 National Alliance on Mental Illness poll.

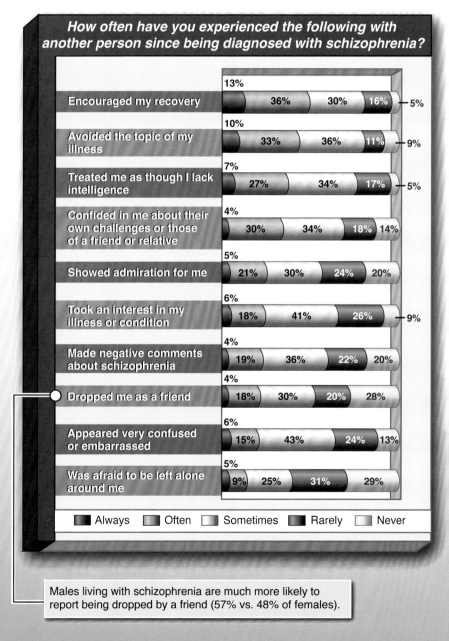

How often have you experienced the following with another person since being diagnosed with schizophrenia?

Reaction	Always	Often	Sometimes	Rarely	Never
Encouraged my recovery	13%	36%	30%	16%	5%
Avoided the topic of my illness	10%	33%	36%	11%	9%
Treated me as though I lack intelligence	7%	27%	34%	17%	5%
Confided in me about their own challenges or those of a friend or relative	4%	30%	34%	18%	14%
Showed admiration for me	5%	21%	30%	24%	20%
Took an interest in my illness or condition	6%	18%	41%	26%	9%
Made negative comments about schizophrenia	4%	19%	36%	22%	20%
Dropped me as a friend	4%	18%	30%	20%	28%
Appeared very confused or embarrassed	6%	15%	43%	24%	13%
Was afraid to be left alone around me	5%	9%	25%	31%	29%

Legend: Always, Often, Sometimes, Rarely, Never

Males living with schizophrenia are much more likely to report being dropped by a friend (57% vs. 48% of females).

Source: National Alliance on Mental Illness, *Schizophrenia: Public Attitudes, Personal Needs*, April 25, 2008. www.nami.org.

61

Higher Mortality Rate

A number of studies have shown that people with schizophrenia have a shorter lifespan than those who do not have the disease, with estimates ranging from 10 years to 25 years. According to an 11-year study by researchers from France, the death rate is nearly 4 times higher for schizophrenia sufferers than for the general population. The study involved 3,470 patients, of whom 476 died. This chart shows the causes of death.

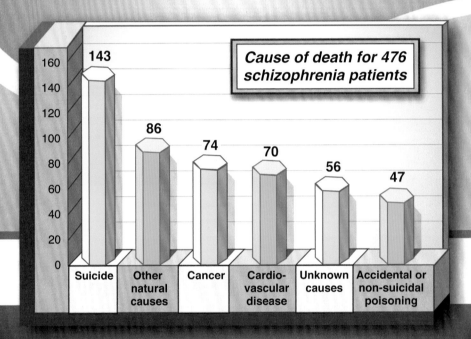

Cause of death for 476 schizophrenia patients

Source: Patient Health International, "Cancer Is Major Cause of Death in Schizophrenia Patients," June 23, 2009. www.patienthealthinternational.com.

- A study by psychiatrist Alexandra Bottas showed that up to 26 percent of people with schizophrenia also suffer from obsessive-compulsive disorder, compared with **2 to 3 percent** in the general population.

The Connection Between Schizophrenia, Violence, and Substance Abuse

Mental health organizations and advocates state that people with schizophrenia are no more prone to violence than those who do not have the disease. That is controversial, however, as some studies have indicated otherwise. A study that was published in 2009 by psychiatrists from the United Kingdom and Sweden showed that schizophrenia sufferers commit more violent acts than the general population, with the likelihood significantly increasing when substance abuse is involved.

Violent crimes committed by people with schizophrenia and people unaffected by schizophrenia with and without substance abuse

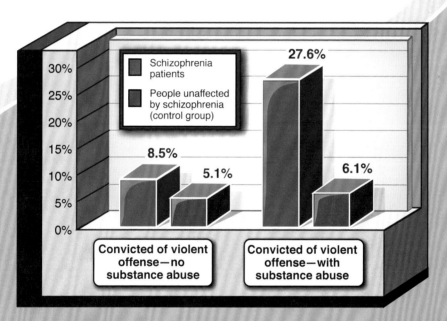

Source: Seena Fazel et al., "Schizophrenia, Substance Abuse, and Violent Crime," *Journal of American Medical Association*, May 20, 2009. http://jama.ama-assn.org.

- According to the National Institute of Mental Health, side effects from **antipsychotic medications** include drowsiness, dizziness, blurred vision, rapid heartbeat, skin rashes, weight gain, and menstrual problems for women.

- According to the World Federation for Mental Health, on average people with schizophrenia **live 10 years less** than the general population.

- The National Institute of Mental Health states that **75 to 90 percent** of schizophrenia sufferers are addicted to smoking, compared with **25 to 30 percent** in the general population.

- A study published in 2009 by researchers from France showed that people with schizophrenia were **50 percent** more likely to die of cancer than the general population.

- In a 2008 survey by the National Alliance on Mental Illness, nearly half of schizophrenia sufferers said their doctors **took their medical problems less seriously** once they learned of their diagnosis.

Can People Overcome Schizophrenia?

> **The outlook for people with schizophrenia continues to improve. Although there is no cure, treatments that work well are available.**
>
> —National Institute of Mental Health, the largest scientific organization in the world specializing in mental illness.

> **A diagnosis of schizophrenia can feel like the end of the world. It is a very serious psychiatric illness, and for the majority of schizophrenics, there will be some symptoms of the disorder off and on throughout their lifetime.**
>
> —Cheryl Lane, a clinical psychologist who contributes to the mental health Web site Schizophrenic.com.

Decades ago a normal life for people with schizophrenia was hardly even a consideration. They were not expected to go to college, find gainful employment, or live independently, much less marry and have a family. This bleak outlook was made clear in a 1964 book titled *The Divided Self: An Existential Study in Sanity and Madness* by the late Scottish psychiatrist Ronald David Laing. He wrote: "The schizophrenic is desperate, is simply without hope. I have never known a schizophrenic who could say he was loved. . . . We have to recognize all the time his distinctiveness and differentness, his separateness and loneliness and despair."[58]

Descent into Psychosis

Frederick J. Frese is living proof of the inaccuracy of Laing's characterization of a life "without hope" for people with schizophrenia. But there was a time in his life when he could certainly identify with the loneliness and despair that results from schizophrenia. During the 1960s, when Frese was in the U.S. Marine Corps, he had a psychotic breakdown and was diagnosed with paranoid schizophrenia. Antipsychotic medication helped ease his symptoms, and after spending time in a military hospital, he was released. Frese went on to earn a master's degree in international business, landed a job at a Fortune 500 company, and felt as though his schizophrenia nightmare was behind him. Before long, however, the psychotic thoughts began to creep back into his mind.

While sitting in church one day, Frese was suddenly overcome with the feeling that some external force had taken control of his body and mind. He rose from the pew and began walking toward the front of the church, as he writes:

> Not long after reaching the priest, in my mind, I began to devolve back through evolution. I became like some kind of monkey, then a barking dog or werewolf. Next I turned into a snake, then a one-celled animal. Eventually I felt myself becoming just an atom. In my mind, it was a tritium atom, the isotope of hydrogen with *three* times hydrogen's ordinary mass. Indeed, tritium is the hydrogen isotope that's split to set off a nuclear explosion. Somehow I'd become the instrument to be used to set off the earth's final nuclear holocaust. I felt myself being put into a large airplane (later I was to understand it had been an ambulance) that was to drop me over Moscow and begin the earth's nuclear annihilation. When I woke, I was strapped down to a bed in Milwaukee's public psychiatric hospital. For a short while I believed that I was in some heavenly place and the world had been destroyed.[59]

After that psychotic breakdown, Frese lost his job and was in and out of psychiatric hospitals for a number of years. At one point in Ohio he was picked up on the street by police officers and taken to a state hospital. During his court hearing, the testifying psychiatrist said that Frese had a degenerative brain disease for which there was no cure and that he would become worse over time. Frese writes: "I was also told that, in all probability, I would be spending the rest of my life under the care of the state hospital system. I was then judicially declared to be an insane person under the laws of Ohio."[60] Yet even with such a dismal prediction, Frese was eventually discharged and was once again on his own.

A Story of Triumph

Frese's life began to turn around when he found a job working for a psychologist in a prison. Upon the advice of his boss, Frese kept his illness and the fact that he was being treated for it a secret. He went back to school and earned a doctorate in psychology, and in 1980 he became director of psychology for the Western Reserve Psychiatric Hospital—the same facility where he was once a patient. That was when Frese began to wonder why he should keep the knowledge of his illness to himself. He explains: "I began considering the possibility that one reason schizophrenia was thought to be a condition from which people didn't recover might be because those of us who do recover don't tell anyone about it. I wasn't sure how many others like me there might be."[61]

In 1995 Frese retired from his executive position and began focusing his energy and efforts on educating people about schizophrenia. Since that time he has traveled extensively and has given more than 1,000 presentations about his own recovery from schizophrenia, offering hope and inspiration to others who suffer from it. Frese is frustrated that the mentally ill are still stigmatized by society, and he wants that to stop—but he also believes that people who suffer from mental illness bear some of the responsibility for changing the negative perceptions. He writes: "For society to begin changing its exclusionary view of us, we have to do certain things to help our cause. To start with, people with mental illnesses, as a group, must no longer be ashamed of who we are. . . . We must stand up, identify ourselves, and be

> "Frederick J. Frese is living proof of the inaccuracy of Laing's characterization of a life 'without hope' for people with schizophrenia."

proud that we have been able to overcome what has been characterized as one of the most devastating of all disabilities."[62]

Early Intervention

Studies have shown that the sooner schizophrenia is diagnosed and treated, the more successful the outcome is likely to be. This was first discovered during the 1980s, when research showed that patients did much better if they were given treatment quickly after a psychotic breakdown. As journalist Charles Schmidt explains in an August 2008 article in *Discover*: "Symptoms were fewer and less intense. Often the symptoms could be controlled with a lower dose of medication than that used to treat full-blown psychosis. Patients also had less evidence of the loss of brain tissue, a key characteristic of the disease."[63]

The importance of early intervention is at the heart of a treatment program called Portland Identification and Early Referral, or PIER. Founded by William McFarlane, a psychiatrist from Portland, Maine, PIER relies on community networks that are composed of clinicians, teachers, social workers, and others. They are taught to spot early schizophrenia warning signs in young people, such as paranoia, disorganized thinking, hallucinations, withdrawal from their peers, and a sudden loss of interest in social activities. Anyone who is believed to be at risk for psychosis is referred to the program.

> "Studies have shown that the sooner schizophrenia is diagnosed and treated, the more successful the outcome is likely to be."

If PIER staff members determine that early treatment is appropriate, a regimen is designed for the patient. This includes antipsychotic medications and group therapy, as well as support services at the patient's school or place of employment. These social supports are an essential part of treatment because they protect vulnerable patients, as Schmidt writes, "from environmental triggers—illicit drugs and emotional stress in particular—that might send them over the edge. Over time, most patients learn how to manage their condition, just as patients with chronic diseases such as diabetes learn to monitor symptoms and medications."[64]

A Changed Life

Camila Knudsen (not her real name) was admitted to the PIER program in 2001 when she was 14. She had begun noticing that neighborhood noises such as lawn mowers, airplanes, and barking dogs were melding together into a deafening, disturbing sound. This explosion of noise made it impossible for Knudsen to hear or understand what people were saying, as she explains: "My mind was a blank. Sometimes I felt like I couldn't see or hear anything. I'd walk past someone and if they were laughing, I felt like they were laughing at me."[65] Knudsen reached the point where she rarely left her bedroom. She avoided friends and often just stared into space. Her parents became alarmed, and based on advice from a pediatrician, they referred her to McFarlane's program. The staff determined that Knudsen was at high risk for developing full-blown psychosis and that quick intervention was crucial.

> " Many [people with schizophrenia] discontinue taking antipsychotics, either because they erroneously believe they are cured, or they can no longer stand the side effects. "

Knudsen completed a four-year treatment program at PIER in 2005. She has made amazing progress, although she has learned from personal experience that she must continue taking antipsychotic medications. Because she was feeling so good, she stopped taking the drugs for a short time in 2007, and before long she started having strange feelings again. Today Knudsen is a very different person from the 14-year-old who was on the verge of a psychotic breakdown. Her father explains: "You couldn't tell she has a mental illness now if you tried. She's going to be a productive member of society."[66]

A Tragic Death

Knudsen's belief that she no longer needed medication is extremely common among people with schizophrenia. Many discontinue taking antipsychotics, either because they erroneously believe they are cured, or they can no longer stand the side effects. This can be dangerous, as the National Alliance on Mental Illness explains: "People with schizophrenia who stop taking prescribed medication are at risk of relapse into an acute psychotic episode."[67] Elliott Carmi, a 25-year-old schizophrenia sufferer from Olympia, Washington, stopped taking his antipsychotic medication on advice of his doctor. Shortly after this, Carmi killed himself.

> "Schizophrenia is a serious, often debilitating mental illness that can significantly impair someone's life—yet numerous people have fought the disease and beaten it.

Before Carmi was diagnosed with paranoid schizophrenia, he had been haunted by voices. The voices told him that other people, even those he loved, wanted to harm him. Once he started treatment with an antipsychotic drug, his symptoms eased, and he began to think clearly again. Carmi spoke fluent Italian and had a goal of eventually traveling to Italy so he could teach English as a second language.

In November 2009 Carmi called his mother, Laura Holgate, to tell her that he was excited to have found a new doctor. During another telephone conversation, Carmi mentioned that the doctor had told him to stop taking his antipsychotic medication. Six days later Carmi was found dead in his apartment from a self-inflicted gunshot wound.

For people with schizophrenia, both those who are on medication and those who are not, suicide is a high risk. The National Institute of Mental Health states that suicide among the general population is about 10 deaths per 100,000 people, or 0.01 percent—and these numbers rise exponentially among schizophrenia sufferers. According to a March 2007 article in the journal *Annals of General Psychiatry*, research has shown that up to 13 percent of schizophrenic patients take their own lives and, as the authors write, "it is likely that the higher end of the range is the most accurate estimate."[68]

"Keeping the Spirit Alive"

Schizophrenia is a serious, often debilitating mental illness that can significantly impair someone's life—yet numerous people have fought the disease and beaten it. Two of those people, Elyn R. Saks and Frederick

J. Frese, both triumphed over schizophrenia and went on to live happy, meaningful lives. Another is Ronald Bassman who, like Frese and Saks, was once given no hope for a future.

After Bassman was discharged from a psychiatric hospital, a doctor told him that he had "an incurable disease called schizophrenia," and that his chances of ending up back in the hospital were high. He writes:

> His medical orders were directed at my parents, not me, and stated with an absolute authority that discouraged any challenge. He predicted a lifetime in the back ward of a state hospital if his orders were not followed. "He will need to take medication for the rest of his life. For now, you need to bring him to the hospital weekly for outpatient treatment and he must not see any of his old friends." I was devastated.[69]

Bassman proved how very wrong that doctor was. Now a psychologist and author, he often speaks to audiences about schizophrenia and emphasizes how essential it is that people never give up hope. Hope, Bassman says, is a crucial element for human survival because without it, patients can lose their will to keep fighting. He writes: "It isn't one person or incident or clinical intervention that is critical for change to occur. Instead, it's a complex process. One essential factor is keeping the spirit alive."[70]

Can People Overcome Schizophrenia?

66 **Schizophrenia is a manageable disease. Advances in medicine, including antipsychotic medications, psychosocial therapy, and rehabilitation, now enable many people who live with schizophrenia to recover and live productive, fulfilling lives.** 99

—National Alliance on Mental Illness, *Schizophrenia: Public Attitudes, Personal Needs*, June 10, 2008. www.nami.org.

The National Alliance on Mental Illness is dedicated to improving the lives of people who are affected by mental illness, as well as the lives of their families.

66 **Since the introduction of chlorpromazine, the first antipsychotic drug, it has been evident that a large number of patients have schizophrenia that is treatment resistant.** 99

—Seong S. Shim, "Treatment-Resistant Schizophrenia," *Psychiatric Times*, August 17, 2009. www.psychiatrictimes.com.

Shim is an assistant professor in the Department of Psychiatry at Case Western Reserve University School of Medicine in Cleveland, Ohio, and a staff psychiatrist at the Cleveland VA Medical Center.

* Editor's Note: While the definition of a primary source can be narrowly or broadly defined, for the purposes of Compact Research, a primary source consists of: 1) results of original research presented by an organization or researcher; 2) eyewitness accounts of events, personal experience, or work experience; 3) first-person editorials offering pundits' opinions; 4) government officials presenting political plans and/or policies; 5) representatives of organizations presenting testimony or policy.

66 **Research is already showing us the kind of treatment and support that can help. And, in the future, early identification and treatment could prevent the illness entirely.** 99

—Donald C. Goff, "Silent Demons," *Newsweek*, September 13, 2008.

Goff is director of the schizophrenia clinical and research program at Massachusetts General Hospital and a psychiatry professor at Harvard Medical School.

66 **Despite a few fairly extensive and complex studies looking at the long-term outcomes for schizophrenia, the fact remains that outcome is complex, and is governed by biological, social and psychological factors.** 99

—Jerry Kennard, "Will I Ever Recover from Schizophrenia?" HealthCentral, November 27, 2008. www.healthcentral.com.

Kennard is a psychologist who is an associate fellow and chartered member of the British Psychological Society.

66 **While there is no cure for schizophrenia at the moment, treatments are available which are effective for most people. Unfortunately, more than 50% of people with schizophrenia do not receive appropriate care.** 99

—World Federation for Mental Health, *Learning About Schizophrenia*, 2008. www.wfmh.org.

The World Federation for Mental Health is dedicated to the prevention of mental and emotional disorders, proper care and treatment for those with such disorders, and promotion of mental health.

66 **Treatments have improved over the years, but the thing that's really improved is our understanding of schizophrenia.** 99

—Eve C. Johnstone, "Acceptance Remarks by Dr. Johnstone," *NARSAD Research Quarterly*, Winter 2008. www.narsad.org.

Johnstone is a psychiatry professor and head of the Psychiatry Division at the University of Edinburgh in Scotland and is internationally known for her schizophrenia research.

❝I don't think we know yet how to prevent psychosis per se, but we have some interesting leads, based on the idea that there is a problem in the plasticity of brain cells in people who develop schizophrenia.❞

—Tyrone D. Cannon, interviewed by Brandon Staglin, "Science with Passion: An Interview with Dr. Ty Cannon," International Mental Health Research Organization, November 20, 2009. www.imhro.org.

Cannon is a professor of psychology, psychiatry, and biobehavioral sciences at the University of California–Los Angeles.

❝Early onset of illness, family history of schizophrenia, structural brain abnormalities, and prominent cognitive symptoms are associated with poor prognosis.❞

—Frances R. Frankenburg, "Schizophrenia," Medscape eMedicine, May 14, 2010. http://emedicine.medscape.com.

Frankenburg is an associate professor in the Department of Psychiatry at Boston University School of Medicine.

❝If effective treatment is given early, up to 80% of individuals can achieve an improvement of symptoms to a level at which the symptoms may no longer interfere with day to day behaviour or functioning.❞

—Janssen Pharmaceutica, "About Schizophrenia," Psychiatry 24x7, August 2009. www.psychiatry24x7.com.

Based in Titusville, New Jersey, Janssen Pharmaceutica markets prescription medications for the treatment of schizophrenia and other mental illnesses.

Can People Overcome Schizophrenia?

- According to the Schizophrenia and Related Disorders Alliance of America, studies have shown that **25 percent** of schizophrenia sufferers recover completely, **50 percent** are improved over a 10-year period, and **25 percent** do not improve over time.

- According to the National Institute of Mental Health, if schizophrenia medications are discontinued, the relapse rate is about **80 percent** within two years.

- The World Health Organization states that **50 percent** of people with schizophrenia cannot access adequate treatment, and **90 percent** of those people live in developing countries.

- A 2008 survey by the National Alliance on Mental Illness showed that there is an average delay of **8.5 years** between the time people first experience schizophrenia symptoms and when they receive treatment.

- According to psychologist Frederick J. Frese, who overcame paranoid schizophrenia, unemployment rates for the mentally ill are as high as **80 to 90 percent**.

- The National Institute of Mental Health states that about 1 out of every 10 people with schizophrenia commits **suicide**, compared with 1 out of 10,000 people among the general population.

What Americans Think About Schizophrenia Recovery

In a February 2008 survey for the National Alliance on Mental Illness, members of the general population were asked for their perspectives on whether people with schizophrenia can lead independent lives and whether the disease can be cured.

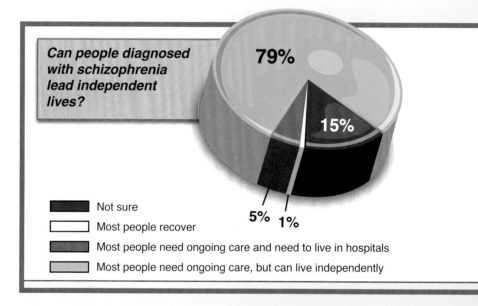

Can people diagnosed with schizophrenia lead independent lives?

79%

15%

5% 1%

- Not sure
- Most people recover
- Most people need ongoing care and need to live in hospitals
- Most people need ongoing care, but can live independently

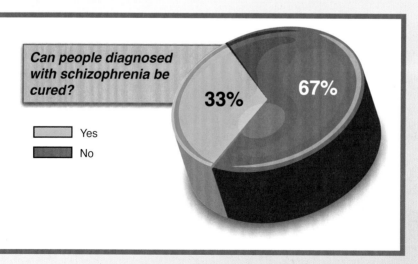

Can people diagnosed with schizophrenia be cured?

33% 67%

- Yes
- No

Source: National Alliance on Mental Illness, *Schizophrenia: Public Attitudes, Personal Needs*, April 25, 2008. www.nami.org.

Declining Research Funding

The National Institutes of Health (NIH) is a major source of funding for various diseases and areas of research. A comparison of NIH estimates for 2011 research funding and actual spending in 2006 shows that some areas of research, such as aging and cancer, are likely to receive increased funding while others, including schizophrenia, are likely to see reduced funding.

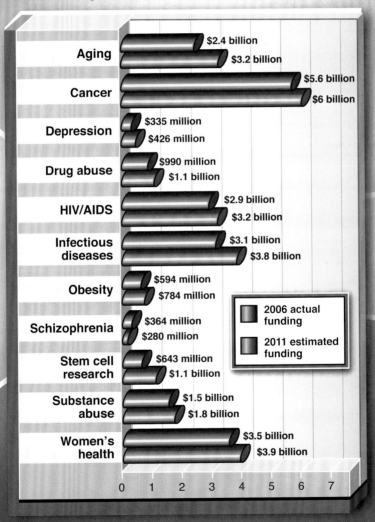

Category	2006 actual funding	2011 estimated funding
Aging	$2.4 billion	$3.2 billion
Cancer	$5.6 billion	$6 billion
Depression	$335 million	$426 million
Drug abuse	$990 million	$1.1 billion
HIV/AIDS	$2.9 billion	$3.2 billion
Infectious diseases	$3.1 billion	$3.8 billion
Obesity	$594 million	$784 million
Schizophrenia	$364 million	$280 million
Stem cell research	$643 million	$1.1 billion
Substance abuse	$1.5 billion	$1.8 billion
Women's health	$3.5 billion	$3.9 billion

Note: Funding allocations for fiscal year 2011 are estimates as of February 1, 2010.

Source: National Institutes of Health, "Estimates of Funding for Various Research, Condition, and Disease Categories."

Key People and Advocacy Groups

American Psychiatric Association: A medical society that represents nearly 40,000 psychiatric physicians throughout the world and publishes the *Diagnostic and Statistical Manual of Mental Disorders*.

Paul Eugen Bleuler: A Swiss psychiatrist who coined the term *schizophrenia* in 1908.

Donald C. Goff: The director of the schizophrenia clinical and research program at Massachusetts General Hospital, a psychiatry professor at Harvard Medical School, and a leading researcher on the role of genetics in the development of schizophrenia.

Eve C. Johnstone: A psychiatry professor and head of the Psychiatry Division at the University of Edinburgh in Scotland, Johnstone is known throughout the world for her decades of research on schizophrenia.

Emil Kraepelin: A German psychiatrist who combined several mental illnesses under the term *dementia praecox* in 1898; the disease later became known as schizophrenia.

Henri Laborit: A French surgeon who discovered that an antihistamine called chlorpromazine eliminated many symptoms of schizophrenia in his patients, which led to widespread interest in use of the drug to treat psychiatric disorders.

Jeffrey Lieberman: A noted schizophrenia expert who is chair of the Department of Psychiatry at the Columbia University College of Physicians and Surgeons, director of the New York State Psychiatric Institute, and director of the Lieber Center for Schizophrenia Research.

Mental Health America: A nonprofit organization that is dedicated to helping people live mentally healthier lives and to educating the public about mental health and mental illness.

National Alliance for Research on Schizophrenia and Depression: An organization that raises money from donors around the world and invests it in mental health research.

National Alliance on Mental Illness: An organization that is dedicated to improving the lives of people who suffer from mental illness, as well as the lives of their families.

National Institute of Mental Health (NIMH): A U.S. government agency that seeks to reduce mental illness and behavioral disorders through research, the NIMH is the largest scientific organization in the world specializing in mental illness.

Schizophrenia and Related Disorders Alliance of America: An advocacy organization that promotes improvement in the lives of people with schizophrenia and their families.

World Federation for Mental Health: An international organization that is dedicated to the prevention of mental and emotional disorders, proper care and treatment for those with such disorders, and promotion of mental health.

Chronology

1724
Puritan clergyman Cotton Mather defies the common belief that mental illnesses are caused by supernatural phenomena and becomes the first to advocate physical causes.

1898
German psychiatrist Emil Kraepelin publishes a paper in which he combines several mental illnesses under the term *dementia praecox*, a condition that is later named schizophrenia.

1928
Austrian psychiatrist Manfred Sakel introduces a treatment for schizophrenia that involves giving patients injections of insulin in such massive doses that it induces a deep coma.

1936
Portuguese neurologist António Egas Moniz introduces the prefrontal leucotomy (later called lobotomy) to be used on patients with schizophrenia. The operation involves surgically cutting nerve connections between the area of the brain above the eyes and the rest of the brain.

1700   1800   1900   1950

1812
American physician Benjamin Rush becomes one of the earliest advocates of humane treatment for the mentally ill by outlawing whips, straitjackets, and chains at Pennsylvania Hospital.

1908
In a lecture before the German Psychiatric Association, Swiss psychiatrist Paul Eugen Bleuler proposes that the term *schizophrenia* replace Emil Kraepelin's *dementia praecox* due to the "split" in psychic functioning among those who suffer from the disease.

1949
The National Institute of Mental Health is established in Bethesda, Maryland.

1887
German psychiatrist Hermann Emminghaus publishes the first textbook on child psychiatry, *Psychic Disturbances of Childhood*, in which he discusses psychotic symptoms in children and theorizes that they are caused by blood vessel disturbances in the cortex of the brain.

1933
Psychoanalyst Viktor Tausk publishes an essay that describes delusions in his patients with schizophrenia and suggests that these delusions are controlled by mystical machines and are out of patients' control.

1948
German psychiatrist Frieda Fromm-Reichmann publishes a paper in which she coins the term *schizophrenogenic mother*, in support of her theory that schizophrenia is caused by a dysfunctional relationship between children and their mothers.

1951

French surgeon Henri Laborit discovers that an antihistamine called chlorpromazine is found to eliminate many symptoms of schizophrenia in his patients. This leads to widespread interest in use of the drug to treat psychiatric disorders.

2010

Researchers for the United Kingdom confirm a long-held theory that an abnormal interaction between the brain chemicals glutamate and dopamine plays a major role in the development of psychosis.

2007

A study published in the *Journal of the American Academy of Child and Adolescent Psychiatry* shows that youth who are diagnosed with schizophrenia prior to age 18 have significantly worse impairment than do adults with schizophrenia.

1980

The American Psychiatric Association releases its third edition of the *Diagnostic and Statistical Manual of Mental Disorders*, which categorizes schizophrenia into its various types.

1950

1980

2010

1968

Schizophrenia appears as an official diagnosis in the second edition of the American Psychiatric Association's *Diagnostic and Statistical Manual of Mental Disorders*.

1987

Researchers from Loyola Marymount University in Los Angeles announce a study showing a link between schizophrenia and prenatal exposure to influenza.

2003

National Institute of Mental Health director Thomas Insel states that with the right financial investments, scientists are within reach of finding a cure for schizophrenia by the year 2013.

1971

British engineer Godfrey Hounsfield creates an instrument that combines X-rays with computer technology and calls it computed tomography (CT). The CT scanner becomes especially useful for looking at problems within the brain.

2006

An in-depth study by the consulting firm Analysis Group finds that the prevalence of schizophrenia in the United States reached an estimated 1.5 million in 2002.

Related Organizations

American Psychiatric Association

100 Wilson Blvd., Suite 1825

Arlington, VA 22209

phone: (888) 357-7924

e-mail: apa@psych.org • Web site: www.psych.org

The American Psychiatric Association is a medical specialty society that represents 38,000 psychiatric physicians throughout the world. Its Web site features news releases, annual reports, research, a link to the *Diagnostic and Statistical Manual of Mental Disorders*, and a search engine that produces a variety of schizophrenia-related articles.

American Psychological Association

50 First St. NE

Washington, DC 20002-4242

phone: (202) 336-5500; toll-free: (800) 374-2721

Web site: www.apa.org

The American Psychological Association is a scientific and professional organization that represents psychology in the United States. Its Web site offers news releases, research, a Hot Topics section, and a search engine that produces numerous articles about schizophrenia.

International Mental Health Research Organization

PO Box 680

Rutherford, CA 94573

phone: (707) 963-4038

Web site: www.imhro.org

The International Mental Health Research Organization is committed to funding research and raising awareness of schizophrenia, depression, and bipolar disorder. Its Web site features an informative Introduction to Brain Disorders section that discusses schizophrenia symptoms, causes, and treatments; news releases; research; and a link to the Healing the Mind blog.

Johns Hopkins Health System

600 N. Wolfe St.

Baltimore, MD 21287

phone: (410) 955-5000

Web site: www.hopkinsmedicine.org

Johns Hopkins is a leading health center that specializes in patient care, teaching, and research. Its Web site offers a list of scientific publications, news releases, and a search engine that produces a variety of articles about schizophrenia.

Mayo Clinic

200 First St. SW

Rochester, MN 55905

phone: (507) 284-2511 • fax: (507) 284-0161

Web site: www.mayoclinic.com

The Mayo Clinic is a world-renowned medical practice that is dedicated to the diagnosis and treatment of virtually every type of complex illness. The schizophrenia section of its Web site addresses the various types of schizophrenia and related disorders and discusses symptoms, causes, risk factors, complications, and information about treatment.

Mental Health America

2000 N. Beauregard St., 6th Floor

Alexandria, VA 22311

phone: (703) 684-7722; toll-free: (800) 969-6642 • fax: (703) 684-5968

Web site: www.nmha.org

Mental Health America is dedicated to helping people live mentally healthier lives and to educating the public about mental health and mental illness. Its Web site offers a wealth of information about schizophrenia, including a selection of people's real-life stories, news releases, a list of resources, and a search engine that produces articles related to schizophrenia.

National Alliance for Research on Schizophrenia and Depression

60 Cutter Mill Rd., Suite 404

Great Neck, NY 11021

phone: (516) 829-0091 • fax: (516) 487-6930

e-mail: info@narsad.org • Web site: www.narsad.org

The National Alliance for Research on Schizophrenia and Depression is an organization that raises money from donors worldwide and invests the funds in mental health research. Its Web site offers research news, videos, news releases, and articles about schizophrenia.

National Alliance on Mental Illness (NAMI)

3803 N. Fairfax Dr., Suite 100

Arlington, VA 22203

phone: (703) 524-7600; toll-free (800) 950-6264 • fax: (703) 524-9094

Web site: www.nami.org

The NAMI is dedicated to improving the lives of people who suffer from mental illness, as well as the lives of their families. Its Web site features fact sheets, news releases, a Living with Schizophrenia discussion group, and an informative section titled What Is Schizophrenia?

National Institute of Mental Health (NIMH)

Science Writing, Press, and Dissemination Branch

6001 Executive Blvd., Room 8184, MSC 9663

Bethesda, MD 20892-9663

phone: (301) 443-4513; toll-free: (866) 615-6464 • fax: (301) 443-4279

e-mail: nimhinfo@nih.gov • Web site: www.nimh.nih.gov

The NIMH seeks to reduce mental illness and behavioral disorders through research and supports science that will improve the diagnosis, treatment, and prevention of mental disorders. Its Web site features statistics, archived *Science News* articles, and a search engine that produces numerous publications about schizophrenia.

Schizophrenia and Related Disorders Alliance of America (SARDAA)

PO Box 941222

Houston, TX 77094-8222

phone: (240) 423-9432; toll-free: (866) 800-5199

e-mail: info@sardaa.org • Web site: www.sardaa.org

The SARDAA is an advocacy organization that seeks to promote hope and recovery for people with schizophrenia and to eliminate the stigma and myths associated with the disease. Its Web site features an About Schizophrenia section, news articles, video clips, radio spots, a link to the SARDAA blog, and a link to the group's signature program, Schizophrenia Anonymous.

World Federation for Mental Health

12940 Harbor Dr., Suite 101

Woodbridge, VA 22192

phone: (703) 494-6515 • fax: (703) 494-6518

e-mail: info@wfmh.com • Web site: www.wfmh.com

The World Federation for Mental Health is dedicated to the prevention of mental and emotional disorders, proper care and treatment for those with such disorders, and promotion of mental health. Its Web site offers a publication titled *Learning About Schizophrenia* as well as archived newsletters, annual reports, and links to numerous other resources.

World Health Organization

Avenue Appia 20

1211 Geneva 27

Switzerland

phone: 41 22 791 21 11 • fax: 41 22 791 31 11

e-mail: info@who.int • Web site: www.who.int/en

The World Health Organization is the directing and coordinating authority for health within the United Nations system. The Mental Health section of its Web site offers a number of articles about schizophrenia.

For Further Research

Books

Patrick Cockburn and Henry Cockburn, *Henry's Demons: Living with Schizophrenia; A Father and Son's Story*. New York: Scribner, 2011.

Lynn E. DeLisi, *100 Questions and Answers About Schizophrenia: Painful Minds*. Sudbury, MA: Jones and Bartlett, 2011.

Michael Dunn, Colette Corr, Pickens Miller, and Claudia Moon, *Our Voices: First-Person Accounts of Schizophrenia*. Bloomington, IN: iUniverse, 2008.

Dean A. Haycock, *The Everything Health Guide to Schizophrenia*. Avon, MA: Adams Media, 2009.

Jerome Levine and Irene S. Levine, *Schizophrenia for Dummies*. Hoboken, NJ: Wiley, 2009.

Kenneth McIntosh, *Youth with Juvenile Schizophrenia: The Search for Reality*. Philadelphia: Mason Crest, 2008.

Rosemary Radford Ruether, *Many Forms of Madness: A Family's Struggle with Mental Illness and the Mental Health System*. Minneapolis: Fortress, 2010.

Elyn R. Saks, *The Center Cannot Hold*. New York: Hyperion, 2007.

Kurt Snyder, Raquel E. Gur, and Linda Wasmer Andrews, *Me, Myself, and Them: A Firsthand Account of One Young Person's Experience with Schizophrenia*. Oxford: Oxford University Press, 2007.

Periodicals

Linda Bernstein, "The Puzzle of Schizophrenia: Voices and Visions That Aren't Really There Are Signs of this Mental Disorder," *Current Health 2, a Weekly Reader Publication*, March 2008.

Marilyn Elias, "Schizophrenics Battle Stigma, Myths in Addition to Disease," *USA Today*, June 8, 2008.

Donald C. Goff, "Silent Demons," *Newsweek*, September 13, 2008.

Virginia Holman, "Not Like My Mother," *Prevention*, March 2008.

Tony Leys, "Crimes Distort Reality of Schizophrenia," *Des Moines Register*, March 7, 2010.

New York Times Health Guide, "Schizophrenia," February 6, 2008.

Shari Roan, "Jani's at the Mercy of Her Mind," *Los Angeles Times*, June 29, 2009.

Elyn R. Saks, "Diary of a High-Functioning Person with Schizophrenia," *Scientific American*, December 29, 2009.

Charles Schmidt, "Can Schizophrenia Be Cured Before It Starts?" *Discover*, August 2008.

Richard Shrubb, "My Quest for the Schizophrenia Gene," *Community Care*, January 28, 2010.

Justin Sullivan, "A Complex Link Between Marijuana and Schizophrenia," *Time*, July 21, 2010.

Internet Sources

Diane Duckett, ed., *SZ Magazine*. www.schizophreniadigest.com.

Jane McGrath, "How Schizophrenia Works," How Stuff Works, April 8, 2008. http://health.howstuffworks.com/mental-health/schizophrenia/schizophrenia.htm#.

National Alliance on Mental Illness, *Understanding Schizophrenia and Recovery*, August 2008. www.nami.org/Content/Microsites316/NAMI_PA,_Cumberland_and_Perry_Cos_/Discussion_Groups559/No_Active_Discussion_Groups_for_this_Site/NAMI_Schizophrenia_Aug08.pdf.

National Institute of Mental Health, *Schizophrenia*, 2009. www.nimh.nih.gov/health/publications/schizophrenia/schizophrenia-booket-2009.pdf.

Madison Park, "Teen Tries to Quiet the Voices Caused by Schizophrenia," CNN, April 24, 2009. www.cnn.com/2009/HEALTH/04/24/schizophrenia.soloist.brain/index.html.

World Federation for Mental Health, *Learning About Schizophrenia*, 2008. www.wfmh.org/PDF/WFMH_LEARNING_ABOUT_SCHIZOPHRENIA_2.pdf.

Source Notes

Overview

1. Donald C. Goff, "Silent Demons," *Newsweek*, September 13, 2008, p. 66.
2. World Federation for Mental Health, *Learning About Schizophrenia*, 2008. www.wfmh.org.
3. Donald C. Goff, e-mail interview with author, August 3, 2010.
4. Mayo Clinic, "Paranoid Schizophrenia: Symptoms," December 16, 2008. www.mayoclinic.com.
5. Dean A. Haycock, *The Everything Health Guide to Schizophrenia*. Avon, MA: Adams Media, 2009, p. 91.
6. National Institute of Mental Health, *Schizophrenia*, 2009. www.nimh.nih.gov.
7. Haycock, *The Everything Health Guide to Schizophrenia*, p. 57.
8. Lynn E. DeLisi, *100 Questions and Answers About Schizophrenia: Painful Minds*. Sudbury, MA: Jones and Bartlett, 2011, p. 17.
9. DeLisi, *100 Questions and Answers About Schizophrenia*, p. 17.
10. Haycock, *The Everything Health Guide to Schizophrenia*, p. 36.
11. National Alliance on Mental Illness, *Schizophrenia: Public Attitudes, Personal Needs*, June 2008. www.nami.org.
12. Jessica Broadway and Jacobo Mintzer, "The Many Faces of Psychosis in the Elderly: Schizophrenia," Medscape, November 6, 2007. www.medscape.com.
13. Quoted in *Oprah Winfrey Show*, "Childhood Schizophrenia Q&A," October 6, 2009. www.oprah.com.
14. Elyn R. Saks, *The Center Cannot Hold: My Journey Through Madness*. New York: Hyperion, 2007, p. 328.
15. Quoted in Irene Wielawski, "Visualizing Schizophrenia," *New York Times Health Guide*, June 13, 2008. http://health.nytimes.com.
16. Quoted in *Oprah Winfrey Show*, "Childhood Schizophrenia Q&A."
17. National Institute of Mental Health, *Schizophrenia*.
18. Jerome Levine and Irene S. Levine, *Schizophrenia for Dummies*. Hoboken, NJ: Wiley, 2009, p. 165.
19. Saks, *The Center Cannot Hold*, p. 168.
20. Saks, *The Center Cannot Hold*, p. 334.

What Is Schizophrenia?

21. Quoted in DeLisi, *100 Questions and Answers About Schizophrenia*, p. xv.
22. Quoted in DeLisi, *100 Questions and Answers About Schizophrenia*, p. xii.
23. Quoted in DeLisi, *100 Questions and Answers About Schizophrenia*, p. xvi.
24. Quoted in Madison Park, "Teen Tries to Quiet the Voices Caused by Schizophrenia," CNN, April 24, 2009. www.cnn.com.
25. Quoted in Park, "Teen Tries to Quiet the Voices Caused by Schizophrenia."
26. Quoted in Park, "Teen Tries to Quiet the Voices Caused by Schizophrenia."
27. Saks, *The Center Cannot Hold*, p. 170.
28. Saks, *The Center Cannot Hold*, p. 29.
29. Saks, *The Center Cannot Hold*, p. 136.
30. Saks, *The Center Cannot Hold*, p. 138.
31. Quoted in Shari Roan, "Jani's at the Mercy of Her Mind," *Los Angeles Times*, June 29, 2009. www.latimes.com.
32. Michael Schofield, "A Father's Journey—400 and Changing Names," Jani's Journey, August 2009. www.janisjourney.org.
33. Quoted in Radha Chitale, "Keeping Jani Alive: The Perils of Childhood-

Onset Schizophrenia," ABC News, July 1, 2009. http://abcnews.go.com.

34. Schofield, "A Father's Journey—400 and Changing Names."

What Causes Schizophrenia?

35. Quoted in Stuart C. Yudofsky, "Contracting Schizophrenia: Lessons from the Influenza Epidemic of 1918–1919," *Journal of the American Medical Association*, January 21, 2009, p. 325.

36. National Institute of Neurological Disorders and Stroke, "Brain Basics: Know Your Brain," August 18, 2010. www.ninds.nih.gov.

37. Haycock, *The Everything Health Guide to Schizophrenia*, p. 27.

38. Sheryl Ankrom, "The Human Brain: How Brain Cells Communicate with Each Other," About.com: Panic Disorder, February 1, 2009. http://panicdisorder.about.com.

39. Heather Barnett Veague, "Schizophrenia and Neurotransmitters," American Medical Network, May 12, 2009. www.health.am.

40. R. Douglas Fields, "White Matter Matters," *Scientific American*, March 2008. www.scientificamerican.com.

41. Haycock, *The Everything Health Guide to Schizophrenia*, p. 16.

42. Cheryl Corcoran and Dolores Malaspina, "Schizophrenia and Stress," The Doctor Will See You Now, 2009. www.thedoctorwillseeyounow.com.

43. Yudofsky, "Contracting Schizophrenia."

44. Quoted in Science Daily, "Mother's Flu During Pregnancy May Increase Baby's Risk of Schizophrenia," March 11, 2010. www.sciencedaily.com.

What Problems Are Associated with Schizophrenia?

45. Jennifer, "Dedicated to Making the World a Better Place for People with

Mental Illnesses," Mental Health America, January 10, 2009. www.mentalhealthamerica.net.

46. Jennifer, "Dedicated to Making the World a Better Place for People with Mental Illnesses."

47. Jen Daisybee, "In Solitary (Feeling Alone, Separate, and Not Measuring Up)," Suicidal No More, June 16, 2010. www.suicidalnomore.com.

48. Daisybee, "In Solitary (Feeling Alone, Separate, and Not Measuring Up)."

49. Haycock, *The Everything Health Guide to Schizophrenia*, p. 7.

50. Sathnam Sanghera, "Schizophrenia Is the Modern Leprosy," *Sunday Times*, February 5, 2009. www.timesonline.co.uk.

51. Quoted in *Oprah Winfrey Show*, "Childhood Schizophrenia Q&A."

52. Quoted in Jay Schadler, Claire Weinraub, and Elissa Stohler, "Girl with Paranoid Schizophrenia Has Urges to Kill Her Mother," ABC News, March 12, 2010. http://abcnews.go.com.

53. Quoted in Schadler, Weinraub, and Stohler, "Girl with Paranoid Schizophrenia Has Urges to Kill Her Mother."

54. Saks, *The Center Cannot Hold*, pp. 330–31.

55. National Institute of Mental Health, *Schizophrenia*.

56. Quoted in Janis Kelly, "Cancer Risk in Schizophrenia Needs More Attention," Medscape, June 26, 2009. www.medscape.com.

57. Sanghera, "Schizophrenia Is the Modern Leprosy."

Can People Overcome Schizophrenia?

58. R.D. Laing, *The Divided Self: An Existential Study in Sanity and Madness*. New York: Routledge, 1964, p. 39.

59. Fred Frese, "Coming Out of the

Shadows," *Health Affairs*, May/June 2009. http://content.healthaffairs.org.

60. Frese, "Coming Out of the Shadows."

61. Frese, "Coming Out of the Shadows."

62. Frese, "Coming Out of the Shadows."

63. Charles Schmidt, "Can Schizophrenia Be Cured Before It Starts?" *Discover*, July 2008. http://discovermagazine.com.

64. Schmidt, "Can Schizophrenia Be Cured Before It Starts?"

65. Quoted in Schmidt, "Can Schizophrenia Be Cured Before It Starts?"

66. Quoted in Schmidt, "Can Schizophrenia Be Cured Before It Starts?"

67. National Alliance on Mental Illness, "What Is Schizophrenia?" February 2007. www.nami.org.

68. Maurizio Pompili et al., "Suicide Risk in Schizophrenia: Learning from the Past to Change the Future," *Annals of General Psychiatry*, March 16, 2007. www.annals-general-psychiatry.com.

69. Ronald Bassman, "Overcoming the Impossible: My Journey Through Schizophrenia," Healthy Place, March 4, 2007. www.healthyplace.com.

70. Bassman, "Overcoming the Impossible."

List of Illustrations

Index

Note: Page numbers in boldface indicate illustrations.

About the Author

Peggy J. Parks holds a bachelor of science degree from Aquinas College in Grand Rapids, Michigan, where she graduated magna cum laude. An author who has written nearly 100 educational books for children and young adults, Parks lives in Muskegon, Michigan, a town that she says inspires her writing because of its location on the shores of Lake Michigan.

5/12 $\emptyset$

5/3   (5)   1/13

12/14   (7)   2/14

10/15   (10)   8/15

6/17   (15)   4/17